The Hop

The Hop

SHARELLE BYARS MORANVILLE

ILLUSTRATED BY NIKI DALY

DISNEP • HYPERION BOOKS
New York

All rights reserved. Published by Disney • Hyperion Books, an imprint of Disney
Book Group. No part of this book may be reproduced or transmitted in any form
or by any means, electronic or mechanical, including photocopying, recording,
or by any information storage and retrieval system, without written
permission from the publisher.
For information address Disney • Hyperion Books, 114 Fifth Avenue,
New York, New York 10011-5690.
First Edition
1 3 5 7 9 10 8 6 4 2
G475-5664-5-12041
Printed in the United States of America
Designed by Michelle Gengaro-Kokmen

Library of Congress Cataloging-in-Publication Data
Moranville, Sharelle Byars.
The Hop / Sharelle Byars Moranville ; illustrated by Niki Daly. —1st ed.
p. cm.
Summary: The intertwining stories of a girl traveling to the Rock and Roll
Extravaganza and a toad whose home is in danger of being paved over.
ISBN-13: 978-1-4231-3736-8
ISBN-10: 1-4231-3736-1
[1. Conservation of natural resources—Fiction. 2. Toads—Fiction.]
I. Daly, Niki, ill. II. Title.
PZ7.M78825Ho 2012
[Fic]—dc23
2011022908

Reinforced binding
Visit www.disneyhyperionbooks.com

To my husband, Barry

—SBM

If you look the right way,
you can see that the whole world is a garden.

—Frances Hodgson Burnett, *The Secret Garden*

Chapter 1

THE LOAMY TUNNEL HAD FALLEN around Tad during the long night of winter and padded him like a brown blanket. But now the earth was stirring. And even three feet down, the young hopper felt it.

Maybe it was the footsteps of people in the garden, or the deep, seepy drip of warm rain. Maybe it was the chorus of spring peepers.

Tad stirred too. With the ancient toady wisdom, he knew days were getting warm and sunny up top. He knew plump crunchy beetles and luscious slimy slugs ambled above.

Tad was half frozen to his center from the long season of sleep. Sluggishly, he scootched upward through the sand and clay and veins of rotting roots. Moisture soaked through his dry, papery skin.

Near the surface, he tried a little hop. But it was lopsided and feeble—just a lurch, really, that flopped him half out of his hole.

Tad opened his eyes. He lay on his side, a tasty meal for any red-tailed hawk that flew over.

Using his rear diggers, he scrambled the rest of the way into the sun. The last little chunk of ice inside him melted away, and he hopped again. Stronger this time. Then another hop. And another.

Thank the green grass for the feisty two-spotted stinkbug coming through the rye! Tad's sticky tongue snapped out, and he blinked three times slowly, using the back of his eyes to push the bug all the way down his gullet, enjoying it. What a fine bug it was, what a good tickle it made. The first bug always tasted the best.

Tad sat in the April sun for a while, trying to catch up with himself. It had just rained, and the grass was such a sharp green that it gave him a headache. He lurched under the leaves of a feverfew plant, catching the drops of water on his warts and bumps.

He put his rear end into the sun, his head under the dripping leaves of the feverfew.

Tad sat as still as the clod of earth he might have been mistaken for. His belly, mottled with dark spots, fooled a night crawler, dumb as dirt, that wriggled out into the open and—*zot!* The slick dangle of luscious worm disappeared as Tad blinked three times. Ahhhh, much better. Bundle-of-yummy was good in the tummy.

The dew melted him into the mud, made his hands and rear diggers happy. Made him awake enough and strong enough to begin hopping home.

But as he made his way through the grass, something seemed to be following him. When he turned to look, there was nothing there. Yet something wasn't as it should be.

His winter sleep had been different. That was it. Tad couldn't shake off the bad feeling of the stories that had crept into his sleep. He had run from a stink-belching monster that shook the earth. He had heard strange music too. Not toadly music, which was like the chiming of the stars. No, this music was like the wind banging things. Like rain drumming the pond.

Ping! Ping! Ping!

And in another scary story he was dancing, but he was gigantic and his rear diggers looked all wrong. And he was supposed to do something really important, but he couldn't, no matter how hard he tried.

Winter sleep was the time to go back inside Mother Earth's belly to be reborn again. Mother Earth's belly was quiet and peaceful, no place for twitching, fretful toads and drumming rain.

What was wrong with him?

He needed to talk to Seer. Seer saw stories in his sleep—of things that had happened or might happen someday. He called them dreams. Had the monster that roared out of the darkness been a *dream*?

Plus, a spot between Tad's eyes burned like fire. He needed to talk to Seer about that too. He began to hop faster, away from the patch of feverfew toward Cold Bottom Road.

4

"Buuurk?" he called. "Anora?" He wanted to find his friends and hop together back to Toadville-by-Tumbledown, where Seer would be waiting.

Where was everybody? At the end of winter sleep, the grass should be thick with other young hoppers like himself, groggily making their way up Cold Bottom Road. And he should have passed a few old toads croaking amiably as they lurched along. Buuurk or Anora or some other young hoppers should be helping Seer up the hill. Tad blinked. There wasn't a single toad on Cold Bottom Road except himself.

Chapter 2

TAYLOR GOT OFF THE BUS at her grandmother's house, as she did every day. The wind whipped open her jacket and scooped her hair up and made the tip of her nose chilly.

An April shower had turned the asphalt road as shiny as black satin. Taylor picked up a fat night crawler who was just begging to get run over. She laid him in the grass and then hurried up the drive.

"Eve?" she called at the front door. Eve was a funny thing to call a grandmother, but that was her name. Even Taylor's mother called her that, instead of *Mom* or *Mother*.

"I'm here," Eve answered, standing on the deck

outside the country kitchen. "I heard the bus."

Taylor stared at her grandmother. She had on muddy boots, and the knees of her jeans were already wet. What was going on? The spring day when they planted the first seeds was so special that they always went out *together*.

"You didn't forget what day this is, did you?" Taylor asked.

"Do salamanders sing?"

"Mud puppies do." Taylor had learned that in science. Mud puppies were the only salamander that vocalized, according to her teacher.

Her grandmother rolled her eyes.

"Did you start without me?" Taylor pressed.

"Not really. Change your clothes and let's get going."

In her room-away-from-home, Taylor shed her backpack and pulled on a pair of garden jeans from last year. She sucked in and snapped the waist, but the tight jeans made her walk funny. She found a long-sleeved T-shirt with pink flowers on the front. Under the flowers was the message *Impatiens is a virtue*—which Taylor kinda got, and kinda didn't. Her wrists stuck out. Then she zipped on a hooded sweatshirt that smelled like earth and leaves.

"Ready!" she announced, standing with her grandmother at the raised bed where they always started. Each year, they began at the lowest bed and worked their way up the hill.

Taylor slid her arm around her grandmother's waist. Her shoulder fit into Eve's side like a key into a lock. Her cheek pressed to Eve's windbreaker, right where her grandmother's heart was. Taylor breathed in the windy smell of her grandmother's jacket and wished she could stop time right now, at this perfect moment.

"When you were a few months old and your mother had to go back to work, I carried you in a sling as I planted."

Her grandmother told her that every year.

8

"The next spring you crawled around and poked sticks in holes. The next spring, when you were two, you almost put a toad in your mouth before I stopped you."

Her grandmother told her that every year too.

Eve fanned seed packets with a flourish, as if she were doing a card trick. "What shall we plant first? Pick one!"

It was a wonderful magic trick, that a tiny dark seed could change into something curly or something valentine-red and white. Comet radish. Arugula. Spinach. Piquant salad mix. Oakleaf lettuce. Bibb lettuce. Curly endive. French breakfast radish.

Last year Taylor had chosen arugula because she liked the chewy sound of the word. She didn't actually eat the green stuff. But *arrr-uug-u-la* sounded like something that might eat her.

She'd picked curly endive one year, and who knew what she might pick next year? But this year she chose to start with French breakfast radishes, wondering if French people really ate them for breakfast. Taylor wouldn't. Radishes were for lunch, with toasted cheese sandwiches.

As she sprinkled the seeds, her grandmother's shadow moved across the patch of garden soil. Taylor turned to see Eve drop down on the bench at the corner of the raised-bed gardens. Her grandmother *always* mixed the seeds into the dirt and patted the soil down. And Taylor always watered, and her grandmother always wrote the label, and Taylor always pushed it into the soil in the middle of the bed.

"Why aren't you helping?" Taylor called. "What's wrong?"

"Nothing. I just like watching you. Go ahead. You can do my part."

"But—" Taylor wanted to do it the way they always did.

"Really, sweetheart. I'll watch."

So Taylor ran her bare fingers over the loose soil, tumbling the round radish seeds into it. This wasn't the way it was supposed to work.

She picked up the heavy watering can and tilted

it over the bed. Because it was too full, water splatted out and splashed up on her jeans, making her leap back. She didn't look at her grandmother. She just scrawled FRENCH BREAKFAST RADISHES on the wooden stake and jammed it into the ground.

When Eve came and knelt down, starting the row right next to Taylor's, the sun seemed to shine a little brighter.

Chapter 3

BECAUSE THERE WERE NO OTHER TOADS around to lead the way, Tad almost missed the toad hole. It was small and hidden in the shadow of a rotten post. He dropped into it as fast as a gnat could blink.

Where was everybody? Sunlight fell through both ends of the empty corridor. Tad hurried along. Usually, on the first day, the corridor was packed with jostling hoppers, ready for spring.

Then he heard gossipy croaks drifting from the Hall of Old Toads. After the silence it was a relief. At least he was just late, and not all alone. But his warts prickled.

Faint voices came from the Hall of Young Hoppers.

He was so late, Seer might have already started the Telling.

Tad passed the nursery, silent and empty, ready for the newbies who would come out of the pond in midsummer. Tad had once wanted to keep his tail and stay in the pond forever. He loved the warm shadows of the water. And he had stayed a tadpole for longer than anybody else that summer. But one morning, his tail had fallen off and his legs had carried him up Cold Bottom Road to Tumbledown.

Late, late, late. Tad raced along the corridor, the path lit by skylights of translucent pebbles. Root fingers curling from the walls grabbed at him.

He stopped outside the hall.

He wanted to burst in. See everybody. Be welcomed home. Ask Seer what the stories in his sleep meant. But Seer would probably scold him in front of the other hoppers for being late. *A toad in time saves nine,* Seer always told him. *Your friends have to be able to count on you, Tad.* And maybe the hoppers would be able to tell, just by looking at

Tad, that he had been restless inside Mother Earth's belly. So Tad eased into the room.

The old prophet rested on a pile of milkweed in the center of the crowd. His prophet hat hung on the bony ridge between his ancient eyes—eyes that no longer saw clouds or moonlight or moths or Tad. Yet Seer saw things that others didn't. Dreamed things that welled up from deep pools. Predicted things that seemed unlikely.

Seer's milky eyes, like two spring moons, settled on Tad. "The last of our young hoppers has finally arrived."

Somebody whispered, "Seer's blind as a stone. How does he know to the exact flicking tongue who's here?"

Tad bounced forward and thumped the ground three times in a sign of respect. "Greetings, Seer."

Seer looked even more ancient this year, the great ridge between his eyes bulging and ragged. As his hands touched Tad's head in blessing, the old prophet jerked like he had touched a thorn. Could he feel the spot that burned behind Tad's eyes?

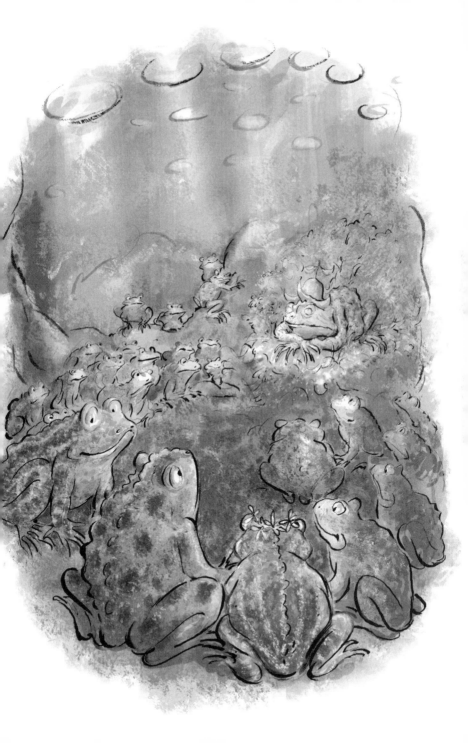

Tad needed to talk to Seer, but not with the other toads around.

Sending up a little cloud of fluff, Seer collapsed back into the milkweed.

Buuurk bumped Tad. "Thank the green grass, toad! I thought a groundhog had got you!"

Tad looked at his best friend. "I just slept too long. How did you sleep?"

"How did I sleep?" Buuurk blinked. "What kind of question is that? I shut my eyes and then I opened my eyes."

"Me too," Tad lied. He didn't want Buuurk to think he was a freak, like the seven-legged cricket they had found in the mulch pile last summer.

Anora, beside Buuurk, nodded. "I told Buuurk not to worry. You do things at your own speed." Her eyes danced in their frames of pretty white warts. Even Anora, who was a summer younger than Tad, knew how he'd gotten his name. Tad was short for tadpole, which was what he'd wanted to stay for as long as he could.

16

Seer righted himself. "Everybody is here," he said. "We will begin."

Still twitchy from his hurry, Tad took his usual place between Buuurk and Anora. All the young hoppers' faces turned toward Seer like moonflowers to the moon. The light falling through the translucent pebbles was soft behind the old prophet as he began the Telling of who the toads were and how they came to be.

"In the beginning, when there was nothing much in the darkness but a smile, Mother Earth and Father Pond found each other."

Tad could hardly make out Seer against the brightening light, but Seer's voice was strong as he told the story the exact same way he always told it, word for word. Tad could practically tell it himself. The next part was how Mother Earth and Father Pond made the sun so they could see each other.

"And they made the moon to play with the sun," Seer intoned. "They made the stars"—Tad's mouth moved along with Seer's next words—"and named each one." Tad loved that part. He wished he knew all the stars' names.

Seer told about the making of the trees and flowers and grass.

And here came the very best part! Tad bumped Buuurk.

"One day, they made a swirl of tadpoles to delight Father Pond. . . ."

Yes, yes, Tad knew. Mother Earth wanted the tadpoles, but Father Pond wouldn't give them to her, so they had a big fight with lots of thunder and lightning.

"In time," Seer explained, as he always did, "they decided to share. Mother Earth pinched off the tails of a few tadpoles and gave them legs so they could walk on her belly. She called the beautiful, breeping creatures her *toads*, her Jewels of Creation."

Tad glanced around at the faces shining with pride. He squirmed next to Buuurk.

"Mother Earth loved her toads so much that she gave them Toadville-by-Tumbledown, with nice rotting wood, a mulch pile, and a garden full of bugs and worms."

A voice cried from the back, "And she thought the toads were so wonderful that she pressed the shape of a toad on the face of the moon."

"Shhhh!" somebody said. "Let Seer tell it."

"She did do that," Seer said. "And to show how much she loves her toads, she takes them back into her belly every year before Father Pond covers her with snow. But she returns them to the garden when the snow melts so Father Pond can enjoy them too."

The creation story always made Tad forget everything except how perfectly splendid he was. Mother Earth and Father Pond's own jewel.

"We are the toads!" a few of the rowdier young hoppers in the back chanted. "We are the toads!"

"And almost all of us came back to life," Anora told Tad. "We counted heads before you got here. Only one very, very old toad didn't make it." She reached out her hand to touch Tad. "Did a mole step on you while you slept? What's that bump behind your eyes?"

Tad ducked, glad that Seer had begun to speak again, and Anora turned to listen.

"We are born of water," Seer croaked. "Yet we live out our days on the land. And we return to the belly of Mother Earth to be born again." Seer's face swept over the young hoppers as if he could see them, but his prophet's hat had slid over his blind eyes.

"And it goes on and on," one of the young girl hoppers behind Tad muttered. "We know."

"Until you roll snake eyes and a blue racer eats you," one of the boy hoppers said.

"Or a grackle," somebody added.

"Or a fox."

"It doesn't matter," Anora cried. "We may go into the Great Cycle, one by one. But Toadville-by-Tumbledown will always be here."

"You tell it, hopper!" somebody shouted from the back.

Why didn't Seer put a stop to their arguing as he usually did? Tad looked at the old prophet. He had shrunk over the winter. A hummingbird could whir by and carry him off.

Finally Seer held up his hand for quiet. "Unless we are bold and brave," he said, "the Great Cycle will end soon."

The sudden silence was so vast that Tad could hear a mole passing by on the other side of wall.

"Rumbler," Seer said. "I told the old toads earlier, but they are like me—too old to do anything about it. Rumbler is coming."

Questions echoed through the hoppers. "Who?"

"Rumbler is as big as many mulch piles." Seer's old voice was frail and shaky. "He has a cry like twenty lightning bolts fighting with one another. He smells like a mountain of stinkbugs."

Tad's warts prickled. Could this Rumbler be the monster in his sleep?

"I have felt his belly on the earth. I have heard his bellows. He will come on feet with teeth. He will scrape the grass off the earth, leaving earthworms and grubs to bake in the sun. He will hit the trees, making them shake out squirrels and baby birds.

21

Foxes and groundhogs will try to flee, but he will overtake them and squash them to jelly. And Tumbledown will crumble on our backs."

Tad put his hands over his eyes, shuddering. Rumbler. So that was the monster's name. Rumbler had been in his sleep. Tad's warts went flat, and the ooze of terror slid out of his skin. Anora was making a noise like a mouse caught in a hawk's talons.

Seer's voice grew more quiet. "When there is nothing left, when Mother Earth's body is bleeding and barren, Rumbler will go after Father Pond."

A hopper in the back croaked wheezily.

"Rumbler will make a sideways hole in the earth, like a woodpecker's hole in a tree, and Father Pond—heartbroken—will slip back into the darkness. And where the hole left by his body was, Rumbler will scoop up Mother's Earth's body and fill the hole. And when everything is dead, humans will lay their covering over Toadville-by-Tumbledown."

"What's a covering?" Tad gasped.

"To be *covered*, to be buried under the sludgy, hardening gray stuff, is to be cut off from the Great

Cycle of life. To be covered is to die forever. It is the end."

Seer shifted his old body until, except for his prophet's hat, Tad could hardly see him against the light.

"We have to do something!" Anora cried.

"I have felt the strength of Rumbler in my belly as he shakes the earth," Seer said. "But I have also dreamed things. Mother Earth and Father Pond are trying to show us a way to save Toadville-by-Tumbledown."

"A way to save ourselves?" somebody cried.

Tad waited. Why didn't Seer tell them?

"A hopper must kiss a human," Seer said.

A hopper must kiss a human.

No, Tad thought. Impossible.

Silence, until someone cried, "Why?"

Humans were uglier than hognose snakes.

"Why can't we kiss a goose or rabbit?" Buuurk cried.

And before a toad could kiss a human, he'd have to catch it.

"A turtle," Anora said. "I might be able to kiss a turtle."

Seer gazed at them blindly, the strength of the prophecy written on his face. "To save Tumbledown from Rumbler, a hopper must kiss a human on the mouth."

"But how will that save us?" Tad asked with dread growing in his heart. There had been a human in his sleep. He remembered now.

"I wish I knew," Seer said.

"What will happen when a toad"—Anora broke off, unable to say the words—"*does that*?"

"We must trust Mother Earth and Father Pond," Seer said.

"Why don't *they* save us?" somebody asked.

"They have shown us the way," Seer replied. "Now we must save ourselves."

Buuurk's warts had all but disappeared, and he looked slick and sickly. "I could try, I guess."

Seer shifted a hand beneath his flabby belly. "Being big and strong is not enough."

They waited for more, but Seer's prophet's hat had

24

begun to tremble with his snores. So all the hoppers thumped the ground three times in respect and made their way silently along the corridor toward the light of the sun.

"You look like you need some sunshine, toad," Buuurk finally said.

Tad could hardly croak. "So do you."

Anora and another girl hopper named Shyly followed them. "Tonight should be the celebration of our return to Tumbledown," Anora said. "I wonder if we'll still have the feast of First Night."

"I hope it isn't the feast of Last Night," Shyly said.

Outside, despite the sun, Tad felt cold to his core. He turned back. "I'll see you later, toads. I have to talk to Seer."

Chapter 4

THE KNEES AND BUTT OF TAYLOR'S JEANS were soaked. Dirt was mashed under her fingernails, and a smear of mud dried on her cheek. From where she sat on the deck, she could see the planted beds down the hill, five in all, where she and her grandmother had worked.

Eve's spring phlox in the neighboring field matched the color of the sky. It was the same color as Taylor's eyes, her grandmother said. Way down in the valley, the new mall made an ugly empty place where a big woods used to be. Taylor got up and moved to a different chair so she didn't have to look at it.

Her grandmother came out with Taylor's favorite

cookies and set the bag on the table. Taylor could taste the creamy grit of the maple filling almost before it touched her tongue.

"Our hands are dirty." Eve sounded as if she didn't care all that much.

"A little dirt makes it taste better," Taylor said. Her grandmother was the only grown-up who understood that.

"Look." Eve pointed behind Taylor. "The pond is shivering."

Taylor turned. Her grandmother was exactly right. The wind had caught the surface of the water and made it shiver. "It has goose bumps," Taylor said, looking at the little prickles of light that dotted its surface.

"It has geese," Eve declared, as three geese floated into view.

There was the weedy beach with a swaybacked dock where Taylor and her friend Kia swam in hot weather, and a dam for rolling down. Today the dam showed pale spring grass, but soon it would be snowy with Eve's daisies.

"Mr. Dennis's son stopped by today," Eve said. "I think he wanted one last look at the place. We walked down to the pond from here, even though he doesn't own the land anymore."

"But we can still use it just like we always have, right?"

"Let's wait and see."

When she was little, she'd pretended to be a princess in charge of her kingdom. The squirrels, rabbits, and deer were hers to watch and name and worry about. Plus she had a big private swimming place with lots of interesting stuff in it. When she floated on her back in the middle of the pond, even the cloud shapes seemed like they had been put there to entertain her. She was getting too old to play princess, but Taylor didn't want to give up her kingdom.

"Why didn't we buy it when Mr. Dennis died?" she asked. "It's always been like ours anyway. Nobody but us has ever used it."

"Couldn't afford it. And what would I do with twenty more acres, Taylor? Two seems like more than enough these days."

Taylor didn't want to think about what her grandmother meant by *these days*. "Maybe the new owners will be like Mr. Dennis, and not pay a bit of attention to the pond and stuff, and it can still be ours."

"Maybe," Eve said. "But it will be their land to use as they please."

"If they're not nice, I think you should take all your flowers back," Taylor said. It sounded stupid, but the thought made her feel better.

Eve smiled. "Well, it's not like I planted the seeds, sweetheart. The birds and time did that."

"Still," Taylor said, "they're your flowers. If you hadn't had them in your garden first, they wouldn't have moved into the field and made it so beautiful that somebody bought it." She sounded like a kindergartener; she knew she did. "So it's kind of like we own the field too," she finished lamely.

"Maybe *kind* of. But my property stops just on this side of the old tumbledown shed, Taylor. The new owners can do whatever they want with the field and woods. And even the pond."

"What would they do with the pond?"

"Not everybody wants a pond."

She saw the look in her grandmother's eyes.

Taylor gasped.

"They couldn't! What would happen to those geese right there?" She pointed to the mama goose now trailing goslings in her V-shaped wake.

Taylor went to the south end of the deck and knelt on the bench, trying to imagine her kingdom without the pond. She couldn't.

A sudden breeze slapped her hood against her neck, and she heard the scream of a hawk.

"We should get out the garden hose and fill the birdbaths," Eve said. "And put up the hammock too. There's so much to do."

"We better hurry, then. Dad will be here soon." And he never wanted to wait for anything.

Just then, the single toot of a car horn said he had arrived. Taylor heard his footsteps on the path, and his voice, edgy, talking to somebody on his phone. He waved hello to both of them, yipped a few words into the phone, and clapped it shut. "Ready?" he said to Taylor. "We've gotta hurry." *Hurry* was his favorite word, Taylor thought.

"I have to change clothes."

"Nah. Just grab your backpack and let's go. Your mother's waiting at Tortillas. Wanna come, Eve?"

"Thanks anyway. I'm dirty and tired."

Despite what her dad said, when she was inside, Taylor yanked off her garden clothes. The jeans had left red marks on her waist. She put on her school jeans and shirt, then washed her hands and face. Her dad was nice enough, but if Taylor sprouted a second head he'd just pay for two quick haircuts without wondering a thing about it. He would never notice that her eyes were the color of the spring phlox around the pond.

"See you tomorrow," Taylor said, finding her grandmother in the kitchen and giving her a hug.

"Not tomorrow. I have the first chemotherapy treatment in the afternoon. They say I'll be tired."

"I'll come over and make you a snack, then."

But her grandmother shook her head. "Thanks, honey. I'll manage. We'll see how the first treatment goes. Maybe the next time . . ."

"But—" Taylor couldn't believe her ears. She always came here after school and stayed until her parents picked her up. And sometimes they worked late and *didn't* pick her up. Which was just fine, because she had lots of stuff at Eve's house.

"We'll work it out, kiddo," her dad said. He gave her grandmother a quick hug. "Good luck tomorrow."

Taylor stalked to the car.

As her dad turned out of the drive, Taylor stared over the valley. The sun was almost down. A tiny clipping of new moon dangled in the pale pink sky. Their car curved around the pond dam and down the hill. As her dad turned onto the main road, Taylor saw a sign in the field that hadn't been there yesterday. PARCELS FOR SALE—ZONED COMMERCIAL. Underneath that was the logo of a company called Central Iowa Realtors.

Taylor knew what the sign meant. It meant another strip mall with another pizza place and another convenience store—when there was already a pizza place and a convenience store just down the street. It meant the loss of her kingdom.

Chapter 5

A TINY CURVE OF NEW MOON hung in the sky. Tad found Buuurk waiting under the leaves of the bleeding heart. As the last of the sun slipped below the edge of the earth, leaving only a dusky glow and the lights from the humanville on the hill, Tad watched all the toads gathering in the dewy grass. On First Night, they celebrated their own newness, although some of the old toads resting under the fern heads were very old.

Seer had finally awakened, and two hoppers were helping him settle just outside the entrance to Tumbledown. His eyes—like marbles that might fall out and roll away in the grass—seemed to rest on Tad and Buuurk. Earlier, when Tad had left his friends to go back and talk to Seer, he had found the old prophet in a deep, jerky sleep and had been afraid to disturb him.

Anora and Shyly were sprinkling dogwood petals in the customary circle just as if Rumbler wasn't out there waiting in the darkness.

"Do you think Anora is pretty?" Buuurk asked.

Anora had large bumps behind her eyes that weren't quite the same size, so Tad thought she was more *cute* than hop-toad gorgeous. But what really made her special, in his opinion, was the large cluster of warts on her back, each one ringed in dazzling white.

"I think Anora's really pretty," Tad said.

"I'm going to invite her to sit by me on the bank tonight when we sing."

"Whoa!" Tad said. Usually it took a few sunsets before the girl and boy hoppers sat together on the bank.

"No time to waste," Buuurk said.

"I know. I just—" He just wished a pretty hopper would sit by him too.

"This year you stick by me," Buuurk said, reading his mind. "If any crawdads come around, I'll take care of them."

Tad tried to puff out his singing sac and look like he didn't know what Buuurk was talking about. But last year a crawdad had chased Tad off the bank. And he'd had to watch the singing from the tall grass. Seer had come by and talked about how a coward died a thousand deaths, but a brave toad died but one. Tad hoped he could stare down the crawdads this year. He was already worn out from winter's sleep and didn't want another lecture.

Seer's blind eyes turned to the sounds. He knew what was going on even though he couldn't see, and he was glad the toads were enjoying life while they could.

Seer remembered being young and brave once. And memory was a comfort, though it was a burden too. Sometimes Seer felt like just one big memory. An old, barely-able-to-hop memory box of all that had ever been.

He remembered singing on the pond bank as a young hopper until he woke up the sun. He remembered feasting on bundle-of-yummy until his belly nearly burst. He remembered winning at ladybug shells. In many ways he had been a lucky toad.

But he knew things from before there was anything. He knew about Mother Earth and Father Pond finding each other in the darkness. And he knew that Toadville-by-Tumbledown might soon not even be a memory because there would be nobody to remember it. The toads would be dead.

In his dream visions, Seer saw many things. Some things were connected and clear. He dreamed of the past and how the toads came to be. He dreamed of the future and how things would be. In his second winter's sleep, he had dreamed the great flood of Tumbledown, for example, but nobody had listened to him that time because he was young and not trusted as a Seer. Many newbies had died when the halls collapsed.

But sometimes the dreams were like moonlight broken by swaying tree branches. He dreamed shapes and faces that shifted in the darkness. Those he had to wrestle to make them give up their meaning. Some of the shapes and faces just seemed puzzling. Others seemed terrifying.

He was pretty sure the last toad to straggle into the Hall of Young Hoppers this morning, the one they called Tad, had dreamed during his winter sleep. When Seer had put his hands on Tad's head to give him the blessing, he'd felt a jewel of dreaming, hot and fiery, just starting to grow under the skin.

Poor young hopper. Dreaming was hard on a body. After Seer began telling the other toads his dreams, the sight had gradually left his eyes. Yet the more blind he became, the more he saw, in a way. And that's when the toads in Toadville-by-Tumbledown had begun calling him Seer.

The young hopper with the jewel beginning to

grow in his head didn't seem to amount to much. Small. Soft voice. Terrified of crawdads. Often late. Had Mother Earth and Father Pond really chosen him, of all toads?

A while later, when everybody had gathered inside the circle of dogwood blossoms, the old toads carried out the delicious-smelling night-smacky-goo. The stuffed slug (because that's what night-smacky-goo was—slug insides creamed with honeysuckle and stuffed back in the slug skin) glistened and wobbled when it was set down in front of Tad.

He took a big serving and forgot everything except the joy of being home. The new moon, because it was only a wisp, made the image of the Toad-in-the-Moon look more like a tadpole.

A glistening blue beetle, so pale and bright it might have been a jewel, was put at Seer's place. It had a pink petal in its mouth, and its antennae were bound with a twist of new clematis vine. The blue beetles, shy, lived in a piece of rotten wood that leaned over Tumbledown. There were only a few, so

only Seer was allowed to eat them, and only at the great feasts.

When everybody was served and seated, and the stars were winking, the Head of Old Toads, a leader chosen each spring for his strong voice and many years of life, puffed out his wrinkled throat and asked for a moment of remembering.

"Remember the things that we have eaten. . . ." he began.

Tad thought of the first stinkbug and the luscious night crawler he had eaten on his way back to Tumbledown and how much perkier they had made him feel.

"Remember the things that have eaten us. . . ." the Head went on.

Tad remembered the red-tailed hawks and crows, the hognose snakes and racers who often ate the inhabitants of Toadville-by-Tumbledown, taking them up into the Great Cycle of life.

"And remember those who have been eaten." The Head named the newbies, hoppers, and old toads who had been eaten since the last First Night Feast.

Tad remembered one of the young hoppers he'd hopped with last year—Bump was his name—who had been eaten by a snake near the mulch pile. Perhaps that snake had died and his body returned to the earth. Perhaps a big hosta had taken nourishment from that earth. Perhaps the very tray of night-smacky-goo inches from Tad's hand was made of a slug who had chewed that hosta. Tad liked knowing that every living thing was part of the great circle.

He was just beginning to feel supremely toadly and content when the Head's voice went all thready and he said something that Tad didn't hear. Then the Head croaked his throat and said it again more loudly. "And remember those who may be *covered*."

The very dome of the night sky shivered, and a few stars fell. Tad felt as if he had been stabbed with an icicle. That had never been part of the Ritual of Remembering before.

A tremor passed through the toads. The darkness suddenly seemed colder than night. It felt like true, eternal death.

Somebody murmured, "Deliver us from Rumbler,"

and it echoed through the gathering until it finally died out in fretful silence.

After a while, the youngest hoppers who had been newbies just last year, began to sing, their voices high and sweet, *breeep, breeep, breeep,* and the stars were calm again.

Buuurk nudged Tad and said, "Eat, toad. No reason not to keep up our strength."

Chapter 6

TAYLOR'S DAD WIPED HIS MOUTH, crumpled his napkin, and stood up.

"I'll be late," he told Taylor's mother. "Midnight, probably. See *you* tomorrow, Peggy Sue," he said, pushing Taylor's nose like it was a button.

Taylor licked the salsa and cheese off her fingers and looked away, embarrassed. That's what he'd wanted to name her. Peggy Sue, after an old song by someone called Buddy Holly. Her dad loved old rock-and-roll music and, on the weekends, drummed in a retro band. And her mother sang in it. But her mother had nixed Peggy Sue. She said people didn't give children two names anymore, and Taylor was a nice non-gender-specific name.

As her dad disappeared through the door, Taylor had a shocking thought. Was it possible he didn't even know her real name?

Her mom chewed quickly, taking little sips of water. Her eyes signaled to Taylor that this was no time for conversation. The goal was to eat and get going.

But Taylor charged ahead anyway. "You're a lawyer, Mom. Can people just go around filling in ponds and mowing down flowers when they're not *their* flowers?" She had to ask. Because what if some weird fact could change things?

Her mother made wait-until-I-finish-chewing motions with one hand and dabbed her mouth with the other.

Finally, she spoke. "Not without the owner's permission. Who owns the pond and the flowers?"

"Eve owns the flowers, and I don't know who owns the pond."

Her mother gave Taylor an *oh, that* look. "It really

is too bad, honey. But I'm afraid the new owners can do whatever they want." She did some texting at the same time she signaled for the bill and found her charge card.

"But it's not *fair*. It's supposed to be ours forever."

Her mother stood up and slung her purse over her shoulder. She was headed for the door into the mall, checking her voice mail, before Taylor even finished wiping her mouth. Taylor grabbed her book bag. "You're not listening," she cried, trotting to catch up.

Her mother turned with her best well-I-am-giving-you-my-full-attention-now look. "I'm listening, sweetie. I just can't do anything about it. Change happens. Real estate is booming out by Eve's place. She could probably sell her house for a small fortune if she wanted to."

Taylor gasped and

stood riveted until she was almost run over by a baby stroller. "Eve would *never* sell her place," Taylor said, running to catch up with her mother. It was *home.* The center of the universe. The place where Taylor's heart lived.

"Sweetie, I grew up there too. And I'd hate to see her sell it. But it's a lot for her to handle. Especially now with everything else. . . ." She shrugged and looked at her vibrating phone.

Taylor wanted to yank the phone out of her mother's hand and throw it into the fountain at the foot of the escalators. Where would she go if her grandmother didn't live there? Who would she be?

"I wish things were different," her mom said, putting the phone back in her pocket.

A little kid walked in front of them with a shiny helium balloon tied to his wrist.

"Balloons," Taylor said, remembering. "I need to get a present for Kia's birthday party Saturday." Not that she was in the mood to shop, but a friend was a friend.

Kia liked stamping, and had about a million

stamps, but there was a craft store upstairs that had maybe two or three million.

Taylor's mom glanced at her watch. "Ten minutes."

"But I can't look at all the stamps and pick anything in ten minutes!"

Her mom tugged her out of the flow. "Taylor, I wish I could just hang out at the mall, but I can't tonight. I've got to leave the office at noon tomorrow to take Eve to the treatment center." Her mother's voice was pinched. "And I'm writing a brief that has to be on a judge's desk before then. So here's the deal: we can run up to the stamp shop for ten minutes—" She broke off to glance at her watch. "Okay, fifteen. But no more. *Or* we can stop at the concierge desk and buy Kia a nice gift card. Then she can choose her stamps herself."

A or B. How about *none of the above*?

"Maybe Eve could bring me here after school."

Taylor's mom sighed. "This is Wednesday. The party is Saturday. Eve has her first chemo tomorrow. She's not going to feel like it."

Taylor could tell her mother's patience had expired. "Fine. A gift card."

Five minutes later, on the way to the car, her mother stopped to dig through her purse for her keys. "So will you be okay staying by yourself tomorrow after school?" she asked. "I'll try to be home by six or seven."

Was that what her dad had meant by *we'll work it out*? What would she do there all by herself?

Her mother handed her a key. "I had this made for you today. You'll be responsible and not lose it, right?"

Taylor put it in her pocket, not meeting her mother's eyes. Was absolutely *everything* going to change?

Chapter 7

DROPS OF DEW, like tiny see-through moons, clung to the grass as the morning sky turned pink. Most of the blossoms from First Night had blown away, but Tad could still make out the circle where the toads had celebrated. He found the old prophet sitting on a rock and thumped the ground three times in respect. "Greetings, Seer."

"I have been expecting you."

Seer inched over, making room on the rock. Even though Tad was among the smallest of the hoppers, the ancient prophet had shrunk so much that he was even smaller. The great bony ridge protruded between his eyes. A place between Tad's own eyes flickered.

"Tell me what you dreamed in your winter sleep," Seer demanded.

Tad almost fell off the stone. "How did you know?" he finally croaked.

"I felt the jewel between your eyes as I gave you my blessing in the Hall of Young Hoppers yesterday. And the jewel marks a dreamer—a someday seer."

"But I don't want to be a seer!"

Seer made a harrumphing noise.

Seers were old and blind. And Tad hadn't even sung on the pond bank with a pretty hopper yet. "I'm more like an ordinary toad," he explained.

When a sun ray lifted over the edge of creation, Seer said, "I had my first winter dream when I was your age."

"But I wouldn't be a good seer," Tad said. "I'm small. My voice is weak." And he was scared of many things—not just crawdads. He was scared of scurrying sounds in the leaves, and of falling stars.

Other toads had begun to stir out of Tumbledown,

looking for worms in the cool of the morning. Tad saw Buuurk under the redbud tree, blossoms drifting down around him. Buuurk was big and brave. Why couldn't *he* have the dreams?

"Mother Earth and Father Pond placed the jewel behind your eyes for a reason," Seer said. "I think perhaps they have chosen you to save us."

Tad swallowed. He didn't know what to say.

The stone beneath them grew warm as the sun floated higher. A slow blackfly droned over Tad, and he automatically zotted it. It made such a fuss going down his gullet with all its buzzing and struggling that he almost spat it out.

"Blackflies are good for courage," Seer said. "Did you know that?"

"I don't really like blackflies." Any other of the young hoppers—*anybody*—would be a better choice to save Tumbledown.

If it was up to Tad to save them, surely Rumbler would come and tear the skin off Mother Earth and chase Father Pond away and kill all the toads. Tears stung Tad's eyes, but he would not let himself cry.

The stone was growing hot. Tad wanted to hop into the shade, but something as sticky as honey held him there.

"Maybe we shouldn't tell the others about my dreams," he heard himself croak. It wasn't a brave thing to say, he knew, but it was better than crying.

"I will let you get used to the idea first. But tell me everything you dreamed, toad."

And so Tad told Seer of the bellowing, stinking monster, though he hadn't known it was called Rumbler. Seer nodded. And Tad told Seer about trying to get something important done, though he wasn't sure what, and how he couldn't, no matter how hard he tried. "See?" he demanded. "Even in my own dreams I let the toads down."

"I am often weak in my dreams too," Seer said. "Eat more blackflies."

Tad shuddered.

"What else did you dream?" Seer asked.

Tad explained the music the best he could, stamping his diggers to the rocking rhythm and croaking out some words about going to the hop.

"Going to the hop?" mused Seer. "What's a hop?"

"I don't know."

"There's nothing like that in my visions," Seer said, sounding surprised.

Tad couldn't bring himself to confess that he'd turned into something freaky and horrible in his dream too.

The two sat in silence.

"When will I have more dreams?" Tad finally asked.

"When you need them, toad."

Chapter 8

"IS IT OKAY TO PICK ANYTHING?" Taylor called to her grandmother, who was resting on the deck. It had been a month since Eve started chemotherapy, and it seemed like she was always tired.

Eve was a garden photographer. Lots of books and magazines had her photographs in them. *Photography by Eve Murphy, West Des Moines, Iowa,* it would say below the picture, which always made Taylor smile. These days her grandmother didn't take many pictures. But still, Taylor decided she should probably ask before she wrecked a flower bed that Eve planned to photograph.

Taylor wanted the tall pink tulips—the ones

that made her think of sunrise—for the May basket she was making her parents. They were at work, of course, even though it was Saturday.

"Go ahead," Eve answered. "If the storm comes, they'll get pounded down anyway."

The air felt like a storm. There was no breeze and the sky was no color.

Taylor snipped seven tall pink tulips because she liked the number seven. The two remaining tulips stood among the heliotrope all by themselves. They looked strange and ugly. She glanced up at her grandmother.

Her grandmother's hair was like the last two tulips. A little was still there after her first chemotherapy treatment a month ago, but it looked strange and disturbing. Taylor had held back tears earlier when Eve had said she was going to shave her head. *I should get it over with,* she'd said. *Bald will look better than dead hanks.* But Taylor had just shaken her head.

Now, feeling her grandmother's gaze, Taylor bent down and cut the last two tulips. She took a deep breath. "It's okay to shave your head," she said, standing up and meeting her grandmother's eyes.

After a moment, Eve nodded.

Taylor drifted down the hill to where the last of the phlox and a few daisies were blooming around the tumbledown shed. They would look pretty with the tulips.

People in hard hats had been around with stakes and surveying equipment, and she knew she was on somebody else's property.

The purple phlox grew wild among the caved-in walls of the shed. When Taylor bent down to cut a stem, a toad bounced, making her sort of scream. They were so startling! She watched the little toad for a moment, frozen near the tip of her shoe.

When she looked up, she saw the man in the hard hat who had been walking around the pond. He was coming toward her.

She looked back at the house. Eve had gone inside.

She knew she wasn't supposed to be over here. Maybe she was going to get in trouble. But she didn't move, even though her heart was pounding.

"These are my grandmother's flowers," she said,

when the man stopped, his hands on his hips, looking at her from behind dark glasses. He had an underbite, like a bulldog.

"You help yourself, hon," he said, taking off his hard hat and wiping sweat with his shirtsleeve. "All this will be gone soon anyway. Does your grandmother live there?" He pointed to Eve's house.

Taylor nodded.

"Well, it's okay to pick the flowers today. But I'm going to be bringing some heavy equipment in here tomorrow, and then it won't be safe to be over here. I need to get the woods down by the road bulldozed first. And then take this shed or whatever it was out of here. Then the big guys will be coming in to get rid of the pond, and this old place will be cleaned up. Shouldn't take more than a couple of weeks, depending on the weather."

His cheerfulness about destroying her world made her shake inside. *Cleaned up?* Did he think she was stupid and didn't understand what was really happening?

He didn't know a thing about how it felt to jump

off the dock on a hot day. How the boards creaked as she ran the length of the dock. How the frame felt warm when she curled her toes against it to push off for a dive. How the cold currents tickled as she settled deeper and felt a fish brush her leg.

"There's a groundhog who lives in there." Taylor pointed to the tumbledown shed. Last Saturday, she and Kia had seen little groundhogs waddling through the grass. For the man, Taylor made her voice sound sweet. Sometimes grown-ups were suckers for animal stories. "She has three babies. The other day she stopped in my grandmother's yard and we got to watch her nurse them."

"Aw," he said.

He was such a phony. Taylor wanted to kick his shins. "So what's going to happen to that family?" she demanded.

"Well, I guess that old groundhog will just have to move," he said cheerfully.

Taylor glared at him over the armful of phlox, then turned and stormed back up the hill.

"Remember, it won't be safe to be over here after today!" he called. "Don't want any accidents with the machinery."

He couldn't banish her from her own kingdom! She would protest! Her grandmother used to protest things.

She pounded up the steps. "Eve!" she cried. "He's taking out the pond!"

Her grandmother came out with two glasses of iced tea and put them on the table. "Did he say that?"

Taylor nodded.

Her grandmother breathed a sound like somebody had just yanked out a tooth. And she shut her eyes for a minute. Then she slipped her arm around Taylor. "I'm sorry, sweetie."

Taylor pushed back. "But he *can't do that*!" Nobody had ever done such a thing to her. How could she have her summer swimming parties? And her winter broom hockey games? That's who she *was*. She would be somebody else if she didn't have the pond. She would be ordinary.

Taylor's heart thudded. She didn't know whether to scream or cry.

"Do you see what I see?" her grandmother finally asked.

Taylor sniffled. "What?" Not that she much cared.

Eve pointed to the deck railing.

Taylor didn't see anything.

And then she did. She barely made him out against the scraggly sweet-pea vine from last year. The praying mantis was totally still, his pale sticklike body about five inches long.

Taylor bent down, hands on her knees, to look. His head was a flat triangle, and little rows of spikes ran along his arms.

"Isn't he ugly?" Eve said.

"Hideous."

"But their name means *prophet* in some languages. The legend is that they point the way for travelers."

As if on cue, the mantis moved. His triangular head turned so he was looking at Taylor. And his body was pointing straight at the pond, as if to say, *Better get going, girl.*

Chapter 9

TAD TRIED NOT TO THINK ABOUT the jewel growing in his head, though sometimes he felt it. He began staying up all night. He leaped into the toadly slick and slop of the mud, and sang until he was hoarse, knowing each sunrise might be the last for Tumbledown. He had not actually felt Rumbler yet, but sometimes his warts prickled with promise that Rumbler would come.

The weather was nice, with lots of warm rain to soak into a toad's skin and lots of sun to hatch juicy bugs. The old toads said it was the best spring ever. But everybody saw the humans with big yellow pumpkins on their heads coming and going around Tumbledown.

"I didn't know you were such a party toad," Buuurk remarked one afternoon as they pulled chamomile that hung over the pea patch and twisted it into sweet-smelling wreaths for Anora and Shyly.

Tad tucked a violet into the wreath. There were lots of things Buuurk didn't know. Buuurk didn't know about Tad's winter dreams or his talks with Seer.

Just then, something quivered under Tad's belly. At first he thought it was a night crawler, and he cocked his tongue for the big *zot!* But it was bigger than a night crawler. Much bigger! The earth shook.

Tad looked at Buuurk, who hugged the ground. Shyly's chamomile wreath quivered and blurred, and all of Toadville trembled. Tad shut his eyes and gripped the grass. Was Tumbledown going to end now, before he even had a chance to try to save it? But after what seemed long enough for the sun to rise and set, the rumbling finally stopped.

"You can open your eyes now, toad," Buuurk said. Tad did.

Buuurk's warts were flat, and there was a pool of terror around him.

"Rumbler," Tad whispered. "That was Rumbler." Tad had finally heard him. And he had survived! "Buuurk," he said, "I have to tell you something. In my winter sleep, I didn't just close my eyes and open them again. I saw things happening. It scared the warts off me." He was still trembling so much he could hardly croak.

Buuurk stared at him. "What are you talking about, toad?"

"Dreams. Seer says I'm going to be a dreamer like him."

Buuurk's look turned to pity.

"I don't want to be a dreamer," Tad confessed. "But I can't hide anymore. I dreamed about Rumbler just like Seer did."

Buuurk shuddered. "The monster got into your sleep?"

Tad nodded.

"Oh, you poor toad," Buuurk said.

Buuurk's pity made Tad feel even worse. He felt lower than a night crawler, because he wanted to hide when he might be able to help.

"What else did you dream?" Buuurk asked, his pale warts saying maybe he didn't really want to know.

"I heard this strange music."

"Was it scary?"

"No."

He tried to sing the song that played the most often in his head, the one about going to a hop. He caught the rhythm and hopped back and forth in the pea patch as he sang.

The look of pity on Buuurk's face turned to amazement.

Tad went on rocking on his diggers and rolling his belly from side to side. He was glad to make Buuurk smile again.

As Tad rocked and rolled, Buuurk began to laugh. He laughed until he was rolling in the peas, holding his speckled belly. Tad could have sung more, but his laughing friend was cracking him up. How could they be silly at a time like this, when Rumbler had just made his first visit? The toads might not see the full moon rise. But still Tad and Buuurk laughed and thrashed in the peas until they were worn out. They sprawled in the dirt, twitching as they hiccuped. Tad didn't dare look at Buuurk, lest he start up again. And if you laughed too long, you'd get eaten by a grackle. Everybody knew that.

"Toad," Buuurk said, sitting up, "I didn't know you could dance!"

Until that very minute, Tad hadn't known he could dance, either. "In the music I heard in my dreams, there were noises like sticks hitting something."

"Teach me the words," Buuurk demanded. "I'll sing, you dance. Anora and Shyly can hit something with sticks or shake pea pods. We'll do it for everybody tonight at Full Moon Eve."

His friend seemed so excited, Tad couldn't say no. Plus, maybe it would cheer the toads up after Rumbler's visit. Word would get around that Tad had heard the music in his winter sleep, and he would never be able to just stalk moths with his friends again.

Seer dozed beneath the bridal wreath bush, having a dream brighter and stranger than any he'd ever had before. He thought for a gnat blink he might have come to the time of passing and would be carried by a crow up into the Great Cycle.

What was this wondrous rainbow of lights far brighter than any he'd ever imagined? What were these enormous shapes glowing in the darkness, one greener than any leaf or blade of grass? Ah . . . there was a sign . . . a giant arch of lights that rushed by him . . . or was he rushing by it? He whizzed under the sign. RENO.

Seer spun and tumbled dizzyingly into darkness for who knew how long. Gently, more shapes bobbed up around him, coming and going, as if both he and they were drifting aimlessly in inky water. Then a human wearing those strange shapes was bouncing to music like Seer had never heard before. Happy music. Hopping music. And Father Pond's deep voice said, "That's your queen. The Queen of the Hop. And if the young dreamer kisses her on time, he will save me and my tadpoles, and Mother Earth and her precious toads."

The voice said no more, and Seer floated in the strange music for a long time until a young hopper touched his hand.

With the hopper's help, Seer made his way into the moonlight, and somebody tied something sweet-smelling around his head. He felt sorry for the young dreamer who would try to save them.

They waited in a silence that made Tad feel tender toward every old toad and young hopper. The sun had not yet set, but already a pale full moon hung in the sky. The Toad-in-the-Moon smiled down on them.

Thumping three times in respect of Seer, who had a purple clematis tied over his prophet's hat, Tad and his friends claimed a beam of the setting sun.

On a cue from Buuurk, Anora began to bang on something round and shiny with a stick, and Shyly began to shake dry pea pods. Tad rocked to the rhythm, and Buuurk began to sing about the Queen of the Hop.

The old toads stopped croaking. A young hopper carrying a beautiful blue beetle to Seer nearly dropped it.

Tad danced and bopped as fast as his legs could go. Anora pounded the stick, and Shyly shook the pea pods until they blurred. Buuurk's mighty singing rolled over the toads. Hop! Hop! Shake! Shake! Rock and roll!

When they were done, the evening was totally quiet. No croaks, no crickets, no cicadas. Tad watched the toads' faces.

One or two young hoppers began to clap, but it died out. Then an old toad slowly nodded, and gradually, like thunder rolling in from far away, the toads cheered and applauded.

Finally, the clamor quieted and the toads sat in a bemused silence until some toad called, "We have never heard such music. Where does it come from?"

Tad kept his eyes on the Toad-in-the-Moon as he confessed, "I heard that music in my winter sleep."

Gasps and murmurs wafted through the crowd. Seer's raspy voice, stronger than it had been for a long time, claimed the evening. "This day I saw the Queen of the Hop in my dreams. Father Pond said the young dreamer was to kiss the Queen of the Hop if we are to live."

At first Tad thought the toads had started to stomp and clap again, but then the sound grew louder. The air began to rumble and the ground began to shake. Something cleared its throat and bellowed like it would gulp Tumbledown in one bite and then make a stinky belch.

"Rumbler!" Tad cried, clutching his friends.

The toads turned to watch the monster come over the hill, its eyes gleaming. In the dying light, Tad saw its legs like giant night crawlers eating their tails. He heard the bellow of all the thunder in creation. He smelled a mountain of stinkbugs. And when he saw the full size of Rumbler, he peed.

Rumbler came closer and closer. Tad felt dizzy from its poisonous breath. He tried to hop out of its path, but his legs wouldn't work. Just as he thought they would all be mashed to jelly, the monster stopped. It shut its eyes. It gave a final stinky snort and fell silent.

The toads waited.

"Has it gone to sleep?" Anora finally whispered.

Chapter 10

AT FIRST, TAYLOR'S FEET FELT HEAVY. But after a while, the May air started to swoosh through her lungs. And then after another couple of warm-up laps, energy was singing through her like a wind. She waved to her grandmother, who watched from the almost empty bleachers. In the six weeks since she had started chemotherapy, Eve hadn't missed one of Taylor's activities.

Once she got in the groove, running made Taylor feel like she had swallowed a happy pill. Like she could leap over the silvery circle of the moon that barely showed in the morning light. Actually, her track coach had told her she was a natural.

Kia fell in beside her, her long dark braid bouncing as she ran.

"So, did you talk to your dad?" Taylor asked.

"Save the chatter, girls!" the coach called from the turf. "Just focus on your breathing."

How could Taylor possibly focus on her breathing when she *had* to know whether their most recent plan to save the pond was going to work?

Kia's dad was a TV news producer. And the plan was that Taylor and Kia would make signs and march around the pond. Kia's dad would come out with a news crew and film their protest and put it on the six o'clock news. The girls would chant things like *Save the pond! Save the fish! Save the toads!* And when the reporter interviewed them, they could talk about what a terrible thing it would be to destroy Mr. Dennis's old place, because it was so special.

Maybe it wasn't special to anybody but her. But another strip mall wouldn't be special to *anybody at all*. It would just be the same old same old.

She glanced at Kia, who held her hand out flat

where the coach couldn't see and made a wobbly sign.

What did that mean?

That she'd asked her dad and he'd said—

He couldn't say no! What was news for if not to report the news? "We've got to talk," she told Kia, out of the side of her mouth.

"Girls," Coach said.

Taylor tried to get her mind on the track meet.

The first event was the dash. "Just look at that finish line," Coach said. "Don't think about anything but that."

Taylor felt a trickle of sweat shoot down her forehead.

The gun popped and she was off. She loved the feeling of flying like an arrow to the target. She imagined her feet weren't even touching the ground—that she was just willing her body to fly out ahead of everybody else.

Maybe she should talk to Kia's dad herself. If she explained it all to him—

And then, Madison McKenzie, the sixth grader from Westcliff, was half a stride ahead.

Taylor tried her hardest, but she couldn't recover. Before she thudded over the finish line, two other girls passed her.

Coach gave high fives and "good jobs," but she also gave Taylor a look.

If Taylor had kept her focus, her teammates would be patting her on the butt right now and telling her she rocked, like Madison McKenzie's teammates were doing to Madison.

In the bleachers, Taylor's parents had joined her grandmother, and they waved. They didn't give a hoot where she placed.

Coach handed out towels and water. "Relays in thirty minutes. Stay warm."

"So what did your dad say?" Taylor asked, pulling Kia aside.

"He said he didn't think a couple of kids carrying signs would have enough impact for a news story. And he said we could get in a lot of trouble too. The land belongs to somebody else now." Kia looked over Taylor's shoulder, no longer meeting her eyes. "And he said I couldn't do it. That it was breaking the law."

Taylor pulled on a sweatshirt and popped up the hood. She didn't want her best friend to see how disappointed she was.

"But listen, Taylor, he told me there's going to be a big city council meeting this Tuesday," Kia said, "and he's heard a lot of people are going to city hall to speak and protest local development in general. The TV stations will all be there."

"Yeah?" Taylor squealed and gave Kia a bear hug. "That will be even better." Lots of people. Lots of signs. Lots of news coverage.

"I've gotta go now," Kia said. "My brother has a baseball game this morning too, so we're trying to be in both places. I don't have another event for a couple of hours. But my dad said I could go with you and carry signs at city hall if you want to do that. And he'll try to make sure we get on camera."

"Thanks so much," Taylor said, hugging Kia

again. "We can make the signs Monday after school, okay?"

Time was running out. It had been over two weeks since the man who looked like a bulldog told her they were going to destroy the pond. Every day, Taylor worried it would be gone forever and that she hadn't done all she could to save it. This was their best plan and it *had* to work.

Taylor climbed the bleachers, where her parents were waiting with her grandmother. Eve had on a pretty purple turban printed with pink hibiscus flowers. Beneath it, she was as bald as a softball. Taylor had touched her shining head this morning, a little embarrassed at first, but it felt kind of nice once she got used to it.

Her mother had on a sun hat. The metal bleachers reflected the sun, making Taylor squint. It had rained in the night, and the world looked scrubbed. Maybe it would rain a lot between now and next Tuesday so the big machinery wouldn't be able to work. She searched the sky for more clouds. It might look a little dark in the west.

"When's your next event?" her dad asked.

"Relays. Thirty minutes."

Her parents looked at each other. Her dad took off his baseball cap and settled it on Taylor's head.

She took it off and handed it back. "You should keep it. You'll get sunburned." It would be a long day, and his hair was getting a little thin on top.

He settled it back on her head. "Your mom and I gotta go," he said. "Wish we didn't, but the band only has three more rehearsals before the road trip."

Well, what did she expect?

Taylor sat beside her grandmother as her parents left. She spotted earbuds dangling out of Eve's bag. Eve probably had a book or two, a sandwich, a bottle of water, an umbrella, and maybe a sleeping bag in there. Taylor could count on her grandmother to stay to the end of all her track meets, no matter how long it took. That was one thing that hadn't changed.

Taylor took off her dad's cap and lay down on the bleacher seat, her knees bent, the top of her head touching her grandmother's leg. She put the baseball cap over her face. It was dark and cozy underneath. They announced the boys' hurdles.

"Eve." Taylor's voice sounded funny with her face covered up.

She felt her grandmother's fingers tickle her bare knee. "What?"

"Is it supposed to rain?"

"I think they said scattered thunderstorms for the next several days. Why?"

She sat up, blinking in the sudden light, and told her grandmother about the city council meeting.

"Taylor, it's fine to make your opinion known," her grandmother said. "But even if it makes a difference, we still wouldn't own Mr. Dennis's old place. You have to face facts. We're not going to be able to swim or ice skate or sled or fish there again."

They didn't know that *for sure.* Maybe her dad would win a huge prize for some building he designed. Maybe her mother would have a colossally big case and make a zillion dollars. And if the pond and woods were still there, then they could *buy* them. But if the ponds and woods were destroyed and covered with concrete, they were gone forever. *FOREVER.*

So they couldn't give up.

"You used to protest things," Taylor reminded her.

Her grandmother gave her a long look, but because of her dark glasses, Taylor couldn't see her eyes.

"My generation did a lot of protesting," she finally said. "I protested the war in Vietnam. I even went to jail for a few hours once."

Taylor gasped. *Her grandmother, in jail?*

"I thought the war was wrong for a lot of reasons," Eve said. "For reasons that other people agreed with. Like people will agree with you that we shouldn't turn the whole countryside into strip malls. But the real reason I stood out in the rain and stared down scary policemen with nightsticks and screamed rude things was purely selfish. I didn't want your grandfather to die in the jungles of Vietnam. I wanted to keep him safe with me always. I wanted that so much I didn't know what to do."

Taylor stared at her grandmother. She sounded so . . . not old. She sounded like Taylor felt. Taylor didn't want the pond and fields to die. Because they were *hers*.

Her grandmother dug in her purse for a tissue and blew her nose.

Taylor put her head in her grandmother's lap. Her grandmother stroked her hair.

"Taylor, I think you should go with your parents on their trip to Reno this year," she said.

Taylor sat up. She couldn't have been more shocked if her grandmother had said, *Let's pierce our belly buttons.*

The Reno week was Taylor's absolute most favorite time of the year. That was the time her parents went off to their rock-and-roll extravaganza, leaving her with Eve. Each day, Taylor and her grandmother did something special, like having a swimming party for Taylor's friends or going to a ball game. Each night, they stayed up late watching movies and eating ice cream.

And then Taylor got it. Her grandmother was too tired this year. "It's okay," she said. "We don't have to do all that stuff we usually do. Really."

Eve took a deep breath. She didn't look at Taylor, but she took her hand. "You need to get to know what your parents do—"

Taylor knew what her parents did. Day and night. Her mother argued with other lawyers, and her dad drew buildings and made little models.

"—for fun," Eve finished. "I would like to see you have some fun this summer."

Taylor blew her bangs off her face. "Oh, all that rock-and-roll stuff. I'd be bored."

"Maybe not," Eve said. "You could stay in a big hotel with all kinds of things for kids to do."

Was her grandmother just trying to get rid of her? Taylor suspected that she was, and it tore out a little place inside. "You look like an old fortune-teller in that turban," she said.

Eve stared at Taylor in silence. Then she smiled. "Then let Madam Eve tell your fortune. Let me read your palm and tell you what awaits."

Taylor swallowed and held out her hand. She was sorry she had said that about the turban. She wished they could back up and start over.

"I see a great change," her grandmother intoned, cradling Taylor's hand in hers.

Taylor didn't want a great change. She wanted things just like they were.

"And I see a journey—a long voyage." She wiggled her eyebrows, and Taylor smiled in spite of herself. "I see bright lights. And a tall prince."

Taylor rolled her eyes.

"I do," Eve insisted, and she went on with silly, extravagant stuff about what all she saw in Taylor's future. "I believe I see you wearing a tiara."

By the time the fortune was fully told, and Taylor had married the prince and become a princess, it was time to warm up with the relay team, and things had been healed between her and Eve. Still, Taylor wished the ugly idea of traveling with her parents hadn't come up. Her grandmother couldn't actually *make* her go to Reno, could she?

Chapter 11

THE TOADS HAD SPENT A RAINY NIGHT huddled under the soft leaves of a sprawling clematis, terrified to go anywhere near Tumbledown, where Rumbler still dozed and oozed a foul smell. One twitch of his enormous feet and their home would be crushed.

Tad was afraid his courage would dissolve before the sun rose, but Seer said all important voyages began at first light. So Tad had waited, listening to the drumming rain and remembering the music in his dreams.

Now, as the sun lifted over a sparkly wet Mother Earth, his own heart drummed so hard he could barely hear Seer's words as all the inhabitants of Tumbledown gathered for his send-off.

"If you make your way to this"—Seer found a broken twig in the wet sand and traced the word RENO—"which will appear in the night sky in colors brighter than the sunset, you will find the young queen. You will know her because she will have this on her head and this on her belly." He drew in the sand again.

"But I've never seen anything like those shapes," Tad worried aloud. He had seen the pale white stems of grass where they went into the earth. He had seen the ball of the sun roll its way across the sky. He had seen bugs and worms and snakes and hawks. He had seen the tadpoles tickling Father Pond. He had seen all of Mother Earth from the top of the mulch pile. "Where do I look for things like that?" It sounded impossible.

Seer gazed at him with his milky eyes. "Wherever there is to look. Follow the mantises. They will point the way."

"How will a mantis know the way?" Tad asked.

"Mother Earth will tell it."

Why couldn't Mother Earth just tell *him*? But that would mean dreaming, and he wasn't sure he wanted to dream. He nodded to Seer. "I'll try," he said, hoping nobody else heard his voice shaking.

His three best friends waited among the toads. Shyly and Anora were wearing purple clematis garlands over the white garlands that Buuurk and

Tad had made. They looked pretty and brave in the morning light. Waiting at home, with Rumbler crouched over Tumbledown, would take courage too. And Buuurk looked as scared as Tad felt.

"The time has come," Seer croaked, motioning for Tad.

Tad was so frightened about going off alone, he didn't know if he could move, but he managed to make his diggers lurch forward.

"Wait for me," Buuurk cried, with a hop out of the crowd.

It took a minute for Tad to understand. Then he didn't dare look at his friend, so great was his gladness that he wouldn't have to go alone.

Tad kept his eyes on Seer, but he nudged Buuurk when they squatted in front of the old prophet for his blessing. "Thank you," he whispered as Seer touched their heads.

"Two toads are better than one," Buuurk whispered back. "Everybody knows that."

"May Mother Earth and Father Pond care for you

both," the old prophet said. He turned them to face the toads of Tumbledown. "May the rain soak gently into your skin. May tasty bugs fill your belly. May the mantises show you the way."

Tad looked at Buuurk. Buuurk looked at Tad. The other toads waited. Tad felt their trust rising off them like a warm fog in the morning air.

Anora lifted her garland from her head and placed it on Buuurk. "Every path has a puddle," she said, the white rings around her warts gleaming in the sunlight.

Shyly hung her garland over Tad's head. "And when the puddle is dry, you know the worth of water."

Tad felt his diggers clinging to the soft grass of home. He would so much rather sit in the mud by Shyly than go look for the queen. But after one last good-bye, he turned and set off, bouncing along beside Buuurk.

They brushed the low-hanging leaves of the dogwood, and dewdrops showered on their backs like a second blessing. As they hopped toward the edge of Mother Earth, Tad could still hear the toads cheering them on.

A shadow of a hawk sailed over them, and Tad shrank into an iris bed, pulling Buuurk with him, waiting among the spear-shaped leaves until the hawk circled wide and flew away. Then the two friends crept out and hurried onward.

The cheers of the toads became a whisper and then only a memory. But Seer's prophecy of Rumbler rang in Tad's head. *He will come on feet with teeth. He will scrape the grass off the earth, leaving earthworms and grubs to bake in the sun. He will hit the trees, making them shake out squirrels and baby birds. Foxes and groundhogs will try to flee, but he will overtake them and squash them to jelly. And Tumbledown will crumble on our backs.*

Chapter 12

TAYLOR HANDED EVE A GLASS OF ICE WATER, then sat beside her in the hammock. Her grandmother smelled like ginger soap, but she also smelled a little like the doctor's office.

"Hey!" It was Taylor's mom on the deck, waving. What was she doing here? She said she had to spend the rest of the weekend at the office.

She came loping down the hill. She kissed Eve on the head, her hand resting on Taylor's shoulder, which she gave a little squeeze at the same time. Then she patted the big canvas bag she was carrying over her shoulder. "I thought we might have a nice lunch on the deck."

Taylor smelled egg rolls.

They walked up the hill very slowly, under the arch made by serviceberry trees: Taylor's mother in front, then her grandmother, then herself. Taylor fought back the urge to put her hands on Eve's back and give her a little push so she would go up the hill as fast as she used to.

Eve stopped and looked at the foxglove bed. "I hate to see grass get started in there," she said. "Once it takes hold, the bed is ruined."

Taylor dropped to her knees, hooking her fingertips into the moist earth, trying to get hold of the little knot just above the roots. "I'll pull it." But the grass was harder to pull than she thought it would be, and came out with a tearing noise. An acrobatic earthworm curled up and wriggled out of sight.

As she worked, she felt her mother and grandmother waiting on the deck.

"Come on, Taylor, while the food's still hot," her mother called.

Sitting at the table under the big green umbrella,

they ate Mongolian beef and sweet-and-sour pork out of cartons, and dipped egg rolls into little clear cups of spicy mustard sauce. Taylor's mom made her stop and go in and scrub her hands when she noticed the soil packed under her fingernails.

When Taylor came back, her grandmother, who had left most of her food uneaten, said, "I was just talking to your mother about the Reno trip."

Taylor stopped mid-bite. So that's what her mother was doing here at lunchtime on a Saturday. Taylor felt her face turn hot. Her mother and her grandmother were ganging up on her! And they'd worked fast. Eve had mentioned the idea to Taylor only yesterday.

Her mother smiled too brightly. "I think it's a wonderful idea, honey. Your dad and I have always wanted you to come with us. Everybody brings their kids." She laughed. "I think our band friends think we're a poor childless couple. There'll be so much for you to do. They have activities and even field trips. . . ."

Her mother was jabbering on, but Taylor looked at her grandmother. Eve's gaze was sad but firm.

Taylor took a deep breath. "Fine," she announced, cutting her mother off. "I'll go." They were leaving the week after the city council meeting, so she would already have been on TV.

Her mother looked so hurt at Taylor's tone that Taylor muttered, "I've always kind of wanted to anyway."

Liar, liar, pants on fire. Taylor couldn't look at her grandmother. Nobody could look at anybody.

As she dabbed up flakes of egg roll and licked her finger, which now tasted like soap and had spoiled the whole lunch, she heard the awful earthmoving machine start up.

She just hoped the man didn't do too much damage before next Tuesday, when she would have a chance to tell the world what he was up to before it was too late.

And then with a flash of understanding, Taylor knew why her grandmother wanted her to go to Reno. Taylor's stomach hurt to think about it. Eve didn't want her to be there when the pond got filled in.

Chapter 13

THE SKY LOOKED LIKE WINDY WATER. The puddles in the grass were slurpy under Tad's belly, and rain beat a rhythm that reminded him of Shyly shaking the pea pods while he danced.

Mantises may have been wandering around in the tall grass, but Tad hadn't seen any. He'd seen only the grass stems parting in front of them and the little white fingers of roots disappearing into the wet bubbles of earth.

They had left Toadville-by-Tumbledown a whole moonrise ago. And now his home seemed as far away as the hawks that disappeared high into the clouds of the sky.

"I didn't know there was so much creation," he told Buuurk. "I wonder why we haven't seen any mantises."

"We might have missed them in the fog," Buuurk said.

A huge crow, inky with rain, swooped out of the mist. Tad froze. But the crow had its eye on something else. It plucked up a small writhing snake from the grass and settled on a fence, tossing back its head until the last thread of the snake's tail disappeared.

As the crow lifted off, thunder rumbled and the light grew dimmer. Lightning crackled around them, making Tad's warts tingle.

"I'll bet we're about to the edge," Buuurk said.

"The edge of what?"

"Creation."

They sloshed on, peering through the mist for a mantis.

Finally, Buuurk zotted a soggy cricket. "Tastes like bird poop, but you can live on it," he said philosophically, looking at Tad. "You should have one too, toad. It will perk you up."

Tad hated crickets. They gave him indigestion. But he did zot a few.

"I wonder what they're doing at home?" Buuurk said.

Longing reached out and wrapped itself around Tad like a morning glory vine and pulled him to a stop. He felt his singing sac quivering. He wished Buuurk wouldn't speak of home.

And then he saw the mantis.

"Look!" he cried.

Buuurk bellowed with joy. "Oh kiss me, moonbeams!"

The mantis just gazed at them, its flat head motionless. Then, as slowly as a dandelion gives up a seed head in the breeze, the mantis lifted its long arm and pointed into the direction of the wind.

"Thank you, thank you," Tad cried as he and Buuurk leaped around in joy. And they veered off in the direction it had pointed.

Tad was so happy about the mantis that he forgot he was tired. They found a clump of earthworms washed out by the storm. Making Tad laugh, Buuurk crammed worms in with both hands until they dangled from his mouth.

By the time the rain stopped, darkness had fallen. The clouds parted, and Tad kept an eye on a winking yellow star, trying to move straight toward it.

He almost hopped right into a fox, sitting still as a stump.

Buuurk saw him too and was already puffing up. Tad felt himself start to grow, getting fatter and taller. The fox leaped at them, his nose first touching Tad, then Buuurk, then Tad again as if he were saying, "Eeeeny, meeeny, miney, moe."

The fox's nose was moist with rain, and the hairs around his mouth spiked out. As his dark lips curled back, Tad saw the teeth, one broken. Tad blew himself up as big as he could. *I'm too big to eat. I'm too big to eat. I must kiss the queen and save my home.*

The mouth was opening, and Tad saw his life back at Toadville-by-Tumbledown pass before him. He peed.

The fox made a choking noise at the smell, and reared back. Then he came in for a close sniff of Buuurk, who was also big and wet. The fox backed up in a hurry, then turned with a pained cry and ran.

Tad and Buuurk sat there for a long time before they were themselves and could hop off into the darkness, with only the stars and an occasional damp moth for company. They hopped until the rising sun chased away the night. They hopped until Tad's legs were as quivery as the pond on a windy day.

Where were they? Except for sky and grass, nothing looked like what he saw from the top of the mulch pile. So now they were someplace else altogether. But where?

As the sun rose higher and they were hopping through an endless stretch of sunny grass, Tad started to overheat. Before long, he would be dried-out crow food.

And then he heard it. The happy splash of water. He trembled with thirst as he pointed. "Look," he croaked.

Birds splashed around in a little pond up in the sky. A fat robin shook, sending water flying everywhere. Tad hopped over to sit beneath the spray, feeling it soothe his thirst. "Let's rest," he said.

Buuurk scootched in beside him. "Ahhh," he croaked. "Thank the green grass."

And when the other voice spoke, they both jumped.

"Who are you?" the toad demanded.

"Whoa!" Tad cried, leaping back. "Where did you come from?"

The toad looked indignant. "Where did *you* come from? I live here."

"Where's here?"

"Toadville-by-Birdbath, of course," the young hopper said. "Where all the toads live."

There were other toadvilles?

Tad glanced at Buuurk, who looked as if he'd seen a snake take wing or a hummingbird burrow into the mulch pile.

"We're from Toadville-by-Tumbledown," Tad said.

"There is no such place." The young hopper looked quite sure.

"Well, here we are anyway," Tad said, feeling for the first time a little bit bold. He knew more about things than this toad did.

Finally the other toad asked, "Well, how did you get here?"

"Hopped," Tad said.

The other toad stared at him.

How many more toadvilles were there? Had he and Buuurk found their way to the edge of Mother Earth? Or was there another toadville or who-knew-what beyond the hedge?

"We're in a hurry. We have to find the Queen of the Hop," Buuurk said. "Have you seen her?"

The other toad looked stupefied. "Who?"

"The Queen of the Hop." With a narrow wood

chip, Tad drew R E N O in the damp dirt under the birdbath. "She's near these shapes. And the shapes glow brighter than the sunset in the night sky."

The young hopper shook his head. "I've never seen anything like that."

He kept looking at them as if they each had two heads. "Why do you need to find her?" he finally asked.

"This toad is going to—" Buuurk began, but Tad nudged him.

"I just need to find her," Tad said. "It's very important."

"I've seen that shape." A girl hopper bounced through the grass to join them.

Buuurk made a sound of joy. "You've seen the shape? Praise the primrose!"

"Is it near here?" Tad cried.

"Not far. I can show you."

Their mission was almost over. Tad began to leap around. He could kiss the queen and be home in a couple of days.

The hopper led them through the privet hedge.

On the other side was another world of green grass and what Tad could only describe as a huge humanville.

As they traveled, their guide made toad eyes at Buuurk. Tad heard her ask him how many toadvilles there were, and Buuurk said, "Two."

Tad wasn't so sure. If there were two, there might be three. And if there were three . . . He was just glad the queen was nearby so he could kiss her and go back home. He didn't really need to know how big Mother Earth was.

Soon they came to an edge of smooth, hard gray stuff. Tad stopped, horrified. He knew what it was, although he'd never seen one.

The hopper bounced onto it. She turned. "Aren't you coming?"

Buuurk stopped too, his warts a putrid green.

"We're grass toads," Tad told the hopper.

"Aren't we all? But you can't get there by grass," she said. "You have to cross this."

Didn't she know what she was sitting on? She was sitting on eternal death. Foulness most . . . *foul*.

She was sitting on a covering. What should he say to her?

"Do you have a seer in your toadville?" he asked.

"What's that?"

"Someone who sees things that others don't." He felt the bulge in his head tingling. "They know what's going to happen. Or what may happen."

"Are you a seer?" she asked.

He didn't want to be one. He didn't want the jewel in his head to grow, to make him see more and more things in his sleep, to press against his eyes and someday make him old and blind. But if wishes were fishes, Seer always said, then hop toads would fly, and Tad could fly across the covering without touching it. But wishes were not fishes.

"We have to do it," he said quietly to Buuurk.

"You first, toad," Buuurk said, glowing green.

Tad put his hands on the covering. It was horrible. Hard. Smooth. Gray with eternal death. He drew his belly over the edge, then slowly followed with his rear diggers, one by one.

The pretty one was looking at him like he had

snails for brains. "It's just a path for the honking, stinky things," she said. "It won't actually hurt you."

Buuurk hopped to sit beside Tad, and they followed the pretty toad across it, Tad feeling with every step like he was walking over the end of time. He tried to keep his belly off of it, to lift up on his toes. He tried not to think about what he was doing. The sun in the sky started spinning around. The covering was hot, and he was getting dry.

"We're almost across," the girl hopper said.

When Tad leaped into the grass, he practically buried himself in it, feeling the soft coolness beneath his belly. He sensed the worms working beneath him and saw a stinkbug weaving between the grass blades.

Zot!

He scootched along, trying to wipe away the dust from the covering. Finally he began to feel like himself again.

After they traveled a while longer, snacking on this and that, the pretty toad said, "We're here!" She hopped up on a rock, and Tad and Buuurk hopped up beside her.

"There," she said, gazing into the distance across a rushing, roaring river of honking stinky things.

It took Tad a while to see it, but then he did. Even in the sunshine, the shapes glowed red. R-E-N-O. They would light up the night sky just fine. This must be what Seer had seen in his dreams. The Queen of the Hop was near. All Tad had to do was close his eyes, hold his nose, and give her a big smackeroo. He felt so giddy he almost tumbled off the rock. His quest was almost over.

Chapter 14

TAYLOR'S DAD DROPPED HER OFF in the circle drive in front of the school. "Pick you up from Kia's at six." His fingers drummed the console.

After school, she and Kia were going to make the posters for the demonstration at city hall the next day. Taylor wanted to make sure Kia's dad knew exactly which posters were theirs so the reporters and camera people couldn't possibly miss them.

Her backpack was crammed with paints and two rolled-up poster-size photographs that her grandmother had helped her with. The photographs were from her grandmother's professional portfolio. One was a picture of the pond at sunrise with a blue heron fishing at the edge. The other was fields of flowers in June, daisies and poppies bending in the wind, the water sparkling with sunlight. Eve had had both of the photographs blown up poster-size for Taylor and Kia. All they had to do was mount them on poster board and sticks, and write messages. Taylor was thinking of SAVE THIS PLACE! PLEASE DON'T LET IT BE KILLED! But she wanted Kia's dad's opinion.

Inside the classroom, Taylor spotted Kia helping Ms. Davies take down the amphibian chart. Taylor waved.

"Everybody! Don't forget to take your amphibians home," Ms. Davies called, then rushed off to settle an argument over Oreo, the black-and-white Dutch rabbit who was being packed up for the summer along with everything else.

Taylor lifted her papier-mâché mud puppy off the shelf. She had made it life-size, about sixteen inches long. She had never seen a real mud puppy, but hoped she might one day. The salamanders she had seen were the little spotted ones that raced through the grass on rainy nights.

"That thing is so gross," Kia said.

Taylor didn't think it was gross. It was interesting. She was going to put it on her bookshelf.

Kia had made a cute little red-eyed tree frog only about three inches long, with bright yellow hands. She slipped it into her pocket. Taylor's mud puppy wouldn't fit in her backpack, so she would have to lug it around.

The school day was short, and they didn't have classes like usual. Just a bunch of last things to do, then lunch and assembly, and then Taylor followed Kia to the long line of cars in front of school.

"So," Kia's dad said as the girls were buckling themselves in, "how are you two going to celebrate the first afternoon of summer?"

"We're going to make posters for the city council meeting tomorrow," Taylor said. Grown-ups sometimes had the concentration of chiggers. Didn't he remember that he was supposed to give them advice? And make sure his reporter and camera-person knew to look for them among the protesters?

"You know what, girls? That got rescheduled. It

came across my desk this morning."

"Rescheduled?" Taylor cried. They couldn't do that!

"Yep. Something about the mayor being invited to a meeting in Washington, D.C. Now the land use meeting is set for a week from today."

A week from today, Taylor and her parents would be in Reno.

She clutched her backpack full of paints and poster materials. This couldn't be happening. She *had* to be at the council meeting. It was her only hope. Surely her parents would let her stay home.

Chapter 15

ANOTHER HUGE STINKY THING roared past, practically shaking Tad off the rock.

"Will she never come?" Buuurk asked. Tad wondered if Buuurk had asked that more times than there were stars in the sky.

They had sat on the rock for many nights, waiting for the queen to appear, but none of the humans they saw bore the marks of the queen.

Tad stared across the wide covering to where the shape RENO glowed brighter than the sunset in the night sky, just as Seer had prophesied.

During the heat of the days they rested in the cool of Toadville-by-Birdbath. The toads in Toadville-by-Birdbath were kind, but they were different. They called their pond Mother Water, and thought the toads had been created by Mother Water and the moon. Tad and Buuurk taught them how to make night-smacky-goo and told them about the wonders of Toadville-by-Tumbledown—the great height of the mulch pile and the sparkling blue beetles, which the toads in Toadville-by-Birdbath had never seen.

"I used to daydream about hunting moths while Seer droned on and on," Buuurk confessed. "Now I'd give my warts to hear his croaky old voice. Wouldn't you?"

"I would," Tad said.

"Where *is* that queen?"

Tad had an urge to knock Buuurk off the rock. If he knew where the queen was, wouldn't he go kiss her so they could get back home?

"When she finally shows up," Buuurk said, "remember to wait for the red moon to rise."

How many times had Buuurk told him that? The warts on Tad's back twitched. He might throw himself in front of a roaring, stinky thing if Buuurk told him again about the three moons.

Tad knew what to do. When the green moon rose over the covering, the stinky things ran. When the yellow moon rose, the stinky things slowed down. And when the red moon rose, most of the stinky things rested. That was when he should hop across the covering and catch the queen and kiss her.

"I didn't think it would take this long," Buuurk said.

Something blazed inside Tad, and his warts crackled. "If you say that one more time—"

"Look!" Buuurk cried, leaping into the air.

And Tad saw her at once. It was a little human, and she was hopping. And she had one of the signs on her head. She reminded him of the newbies, falling down and veering into the grass on their way up Cold Bottom Road. She was practically still a tadpole.

"That's her!" Buuurk said. "Let's go!"

"Let's go!" Tad sprang off the rock and into the grass. "The red moon is rising." And with his first leap he asked the question he'd asked himself so many times.

What would happen when he kissed her? It would save Mother Earth and Father Pond and the toads at home. But what would happen to *him*?

On his third hop toward the covering, Tad heard a noise like a grass cutting thing, only not quite as loud. But the thing was speeding toward them, and it was slinging out a blizzard of white stuff.

"Look out!" He lunged at Buuurk, knocking him out of the path.

The wheels of the thing passed within a toad's length of them, almost mashing them into the dirt.

When Tad climbed off Buuurk, Tad was covered with white stuff. It smelled terrible.

"Hack-a-mana!" Buuurk cried. "What was that?"

Tad yelled, "Here it comes again!" The thing, with a human standing on it, had whirled around and was headed straight at them, still flinging the pellets into the air. The two toads leaped into the bushes. White stuff hailed against the leaves.

Tad felt his eyes swelling shut. His back stung like the sun had exploded on him.

"Are you okay?" Buuurk asked.

Tad felt like any second he might throw up all the aphids he'd eaten today. But he nodded.

"Then you have to cross the covering. Now! Before she gets away."

The queen was there and they'd waited so long.

"I'm okay," Tad said. "I can do it." He took a hop onto the covering. The aphids swirled in his stomach, and he toppled onto his side. He tried to get up, but his diggers wouldn't work. He lay there, fighting off the darkness. He had to catch the queen and kiss her. He had to. But the darkness was stronger than he was, and it finally won.

When Tad woke up, he felt something moist and soft moving along his back, over the warts and bumps behind his eyes, down his face, and across the tops of his hands. He felt as if he had been peeled.

He opened his eyes.

"Rest," a young hopper said. "We're trying to help you."

An old toad handed the hopper a fresh rose petal.

She dipped it in an acorn-cap bowl and went back to rubbing Tad.

He tumbled into darkness again.

When he next opened his eyes, the girl hopper was gone, but Tad could tell he was better. The old toad who'd been there earlier had a boy hopper with him now. They gazed at Tad solemnly.

Was it day or night? Where was Buuurk? Where was the queen? He had to kiss the queen! He tried a hop.

"Easy now. You got a dose of evil snow," the old toad said. "But you're going to be okay. Evil snow makes the yellow flowers die. It makes the toads die sometimes. Thank the Toad-in-the-Moon you're still here! We thought it was snake eyes for you."

"Where's my friend?" Tad asked. *Where was the queen?*

"He got you back here," the old toad answered. "Then he went to get the queen."

The young hopper who had sat silently until now said, "Your friend was very brave."

It took Tad a few heartbeats to begin to make out the meaning of those words. He didn't fully understand until he heard Seer's voice in his head. *A coward dies a thousand deaths. A brave toad dies but one.*

Tad wished he had the pain of the burning evil snow back, so it could twine with the pain in his heart. He shut his eyes and sat very still. He wanted the old toad and young hopper to go away.

After a while, they did.

He sat in the darkness. He could still smell the sweetness of the rose petals they'd used to wash him. He felt the earth quiver a little beneath his belly as the toads of Toadville-by-Birdbath went about their business.

As soon as he could carry the weight of his sadness, he set out for the rock. The sky was turning from dark to light. A mist was falling.

When he scrambled up onto the rock and perched in his old place, he felt like the world had been cleaved in half and he had been left standing unbearably lonely on the edge. And the queen was gone.

A crow, cawing at the roaring stinky things

that threatened its breakfast, was making a meal of Buuurk. A few times, the crow flew angrily away, then returned with a flap of black wings and hovered over the remains of Buuurk's body, taking it up into the Great Cycle.

When the crow was gone, Tad sat for a while in the drizzle before he made his way back to Toadville-by-Birdbath.

The next evening, they feasted in Buuurk's honor. The Head Toad led them in the ritual of remembering that was much like it was at home. Tad's heart felt crushed by his longing for Seer and Shyly and Anora. If they were still living and if he made it home alive, he would tell them Buuurk had given his life to try to catch the queen.

"Remember the things that we have eaten," the Head Toad croaked.

Tad had eaten very little today, but he remembered the aphids.

"Remember the things that have eaten us."

Tad remembered the crow with gratitude. The big black bird had quickly taken up his friend into the eternal cycle of life.

"And remember those who have been eaten. Especially the brave young hopper, Buuurk."

Tad felt the pain squeeze his heart until he thought he might faint. He had to get some air.

He hopped into the darkness.

He nearly fell over the praying mantis standing in the pouring rain. It gazed at Tad. With a slow movement of its long arm, it pointed. And it pointed *away* from the RENO shape.

What should he do?

Seer said to follow the direction the mantises pointed.

Feeling like only half a toad, he hopped through the night, trying to keep his bearings. Did he have the courage to go on alone? Mother Earth was so much bigger than he'd ever imagined.

Tad almost crashed into the second mantis. Its bridgework body dripped. It gazed at Tad and pointed. Tad veered off that way, but his heart wasn't in it. Alone, he would never find the queen. Next spring, the toads wouldn't come back.

Tad came to another covering, which was streaming with roaring stinky things. But there was a third mantis. And he was pointing at something.

It was a roaring stinky thing only a few hops away across the grass. It was very big and, like a turtle, it carried its shell on its back. It was sleeping. Humans were carrying things into its shell.

The mantis moved its arm around in a circle and, once again, pointed to the home on the thing's back as if to say, *How many times do I have to show you?*

Tad was supposed to get in it.

Chapter 16

TAYLOR HEARD RAIN running in the downspout outside her bedroom windows as she packed. Her wish for rain had come true, but it wouldn't last forever. And she wouldn't get to march with the protesters. When she got home, the pond would probably be gone.

How would she be able to look at the space where everything had once been?

Her mother stepped in and dropped some clean laundry on her bed. "Did I see your bike outside in the drive?" she asked.

"Sorry." Taylor rain downstairs and out the back door, through the open garage.

The wet concrete felt cool beneath her bare feet.

She hoped she didn't step on any night crawlers. She righted her bike and rolled it into the garage, and then she went back out. Taylor liked standing in the rain. It was salamander weather.

A van with *Ryan and the Rompers* painted on the side stopped in front, reversed, and backed into their drive.

"Hi," a man said, getting out of the van and smiling at her. Raindrops blossomed on the bill of his baseball cap. "You the lead singer?"

What was he talking about?

Her dad came out the back door carrying parts of his drum set. "Hey, Ron. You know Peggy Sue?"

"Don't believe so," the man said, sticking out his hand. "Ron Waters. Guitar."

Taylor wondered if she should tell him her name wasn't Peggy Sue, but she didn't want to embarrass her dad. "Hello," she said, shaking the man's hand.

The men opened the van and Taylor saw sound equipment, boxes, tripods, and all kinds of musical stuff. Her dad wrapped his drum set in blankets and wedged it into place.

"See you in Reno," he said, sliding the door shut and clapping Ron on the back.

As the van pulled away, her dad's cell phone chimed, and to Taylor's surprise he didn't answer or even look to see who was calling. He just pushed a button and it went quiet. She'd *never* seen him do that.

"You ready to rock and roll?" he asked Taylor.

She stared at him. He looked different. Fluffier. His face wasn't scrunched up.

And he was gazing at her as if he were counting the petals on a flower. "So how come you've never come with us before?" he asked.

Didn't he know the first thing about her?

"I like to stay here."

He nodded. "Right." He put his arm around her shoulders. "But here will still be here when we get back."

Not all of it. That's what was so terrible.

Maybe it was just the misty clouds making the light weird, but Taylor felt something scary brush her heart.

She'd begged to stay home. Just this year, she'd promised her parents. She'd go next year and every year for the rest of her life if she could just stay home this year. But her grandmother was in the hospital for a few days. "To get built back up a little," she'd told Taylor. Nothing to worry about. And Kia was at camp. So there was nobody for Taylor to stay with.

She followed her dad back inside. In the kitchen, on the island counter was a pile of laptops, BlackBerrys, pagers, and iPods. Her dad put his cell phone in with the rest and called upstairs, "Meg? You ready?"

As her mother's footsteps moved overhead, her dad said, "You've never witnessed The Great Turning Off."

Taylor's mom came into the room wearing an old pair of sweats, her hair still damp from the shower. Her parents high-fived, bumped each other's hips, and began turning off everything on the counter. With a series of dying notes, beeps, hums, and sign-off ringtones, all the lights went out and the lids went down.

"There," Taylor's mom said with a sigh. "Isn't that

nice? We'll just bring along our personal phones so we can call each other and Eve."

Her parents linked fingers and swung their hands kind of like Taylor and Kia did sometimes at the mall when they were having a lot of fun.

It was extremely weird.

A while later, when she was supposed to be finishing packing, Taylor sat on her bed and opened the scrapbook that her grandmother had given her when they'd said good-bye. Some of the photos were cracked, and the newspaper clippings were yellow with age.

The first page had a formal portrait of a fat, bald, toothless infant in a little ruffled dress. *Me as a baby,* Eve had written below the picture. *And now I'm bald again.* She had made a smiley face.

Then there were a few snapshots of Eve growing up. One when she was about Taylor's age, standing on the sidewalk with a girlfriend. One in front of a Christmas tree with a young man in hippie clothes. *The first Christmas Ryan and I were married,* the caption said. Taylor had to peer at the picture of the woman with the long, wavy hair and bell-bottom jeans to find any trace of the grandmother she knew.

Then there were pages and pages of clippings about the bands her grandfather had played in. Local papers with stories about their own Ryan Murphy going to Nashville. His band—Ryan and the Rompers. Places they'd played. Clippings from newspapers in Detroit and Dallas and Shreveport. A clipping about a recording contract.

Then a picture of him in a uniform with a duffel bag slung over his shoulder. He had his hand up to shield his face from the sun, and Taylor couldn't see his eyes.

Then his obituary.

Now Taylor knew why her grandmother had cried. And how she knew about protests. And why she understood about people and things going away forever no matter what you did.

Then there was a picture of Eve, her long hair half hiding her face, gazing down at a baby in a pink blanket. *Megan Ryan Murphy, born November 15, 1965.*

"What are you up to?" Taylor's mother asked.

Taylor wished her mom wouldn't sneak up on her.

"Oh, that's me," her mom said. She dropped a stack of folded towels on the foot of Taylor's bed. "Let's see," she said, sitting down.

Taylor scooted over, making room.

"Come and see this, Jim," her mother called.

Taylor's mother reached across her, turning pages. Taylor felt her mother's breath on her neck. "I thought my dad was the handsomest, most magical person who had ever lived. Of course I never even met him. Still . . ." She paged back to a newspaper clipping that showed Ryan Murphy in front of a microphone, cradling a small, sleek guitar, his head thrown back as he sang. "Wasn't he something?"

Before Taylor knew it, the book was on her mom's lap and she was paging ahead.

"This is where I met your dad," she said, pointing to a newspaper story about a reunion of rock-and-roll bands. "Mom took me when I was seventeen. Right here, in this hotel, in the ballroom when they were playing 'Lollipop.'"

"Who said *lollipop*?" Taylor's dad demanded from the doorway.

"I was just showing Taylor the place where we met. I didn't know Eve had kept all this old stuff. Remember the first time we danced?"

Her dad started to hum and sort of rock around. Her mom got off the bed and they touched fingertips, their arms bent, smiling at each other, and then her mother sang some silly words.

Taylor put her pillow over her face. She couldn't stand it. Had her parents been taken over by alien beings? How would she ever survive a whole week in Reno with them?

Chapter 17

FROM A DEEP SHADOW inside the stinky thing's turtle shell, Tad watched humans tromp back and forth carrying things that smelled like home. The fragrance of carrots, potatoes, thyme, and damp earth made him so homesick he shriveled up to almost nothing. As the humans went in and out of the giant turtle shell, they made noises to each other. Their noise wasn't as pretty as birdsong, but better than squirrel jabber or dog talk.

Before long, the turtle shell went dark—so dark he could not see his own hands. Then something rumbled beneath his belly. The stinky thing was waking up and starting to move. Tad crouched, still as stone.

Where was the roaring stinky thing going?

After a while, Tad crept over the trembling bottom. Through a crack in the shell, he saw great snakes of light, the white snakes chasing him, the red snakes racing away from him. Shapes flashed by in the rain. Everything was covered.

He was getting farther and farther from the RENO shape, where he had seen the queen. And he was getting deeper into the covering.

He thought about leaping out of the giant shell. The crack was big enough. But he was very high up, plus he would leap into the snakes of fast light.

Tad backed away from the crack.

It was so cold that his warts hurt and his rear diggers started to go numb. He hopped around, trying to keep warm.

The song from his dreams, the one that had made Buuurk roll in the peas laughing so long ago, popped into his head. He swayed back and forth on his diggers, belting out a few words. But without Buuurk, it wasn't fun. Tad just felt even sadder than before. His voice trailed off until it was a whisper, and he stood silently, shivering.

Behind a box, he found a sluggish grasshopper and a cold fly. He stared out the crack again, feeling the chill of the air.

He had to find a place to burrow before he froze to death.

The stinky thing jolted, flinging Tad into the air. When he landed, he was among carrots, their tops tickling his back. And the carrots were buried in something like dirt. It didn't smell exactly like dirt, but his diggers could make a little tunnel that he could back into.

He stayed among the carrots, half frozen, for what seemed like forever. Sometimes, to prove to himself that he could still move, he left his burrow to peer out of the crack in the turtle shell. When it was light, he saw a wide golden body of water sparkling in the sun. He watched as the stinky thing followed along its edge for a very long time. Finally, heavy with cold and loneliness, Tad went back to his burrow and slept again.

The next time he awoke, he wondered where Buuurk was. And then he remembered. Trembling, he crossed the turtle-shell bottom to peer through the crack again. To his amazement, he saw mulch piles so tall they reached into the clouds, and big animals with horns eating grass.

Over and over, he dozed among the carrots and returned to peek at creation. In places, Mother Earth's body was full of painful-looking cracks. In other places, she was all sand piles. Once, far off, Tad saw giant twisted rocks, like fantastical beasts, rising into the sky. He saw strange squirrel-like animals popping in and out of holes in the ground.

He had no idea Mother Earth was so big and had such amazing animals wandering over her. If Buuurk were here beside him, they could marvel at these strange things together. If Buuurk were here beside him, Tad would feel brave.

Chapter 18

"SAY HELLO TO RENO!" her dad said as their car passed under the sign that arched over the street.

"Hello, Reno!" her mother sang.

"Hello, Reno," Taylor mumbled, feeling a little weird talking to a town.

"Such a friendly sign," her dad sad. "Friendly town too."

"Look, Taylor. There's our hotel." Her mother pointed ahead where two tall towers and a connecting crosswalk made a giant white H against the blue sky.

"It's so big." She thought of things that began with H. Horoscope. Hiccup. Hack. Hop. Homesick.

As she followed her parents into the vast glass-and-marble lobby, she looked up at the colorful silk banners that moved like clouds on a breezy day.

"Over here," her dad said, herding Taylor and her mother toward a large sign that said WELCOME 30TH ANNUAL ROCK AND ROLL EXTRAVAGANZA.

Her mother saw somebody she knew, and picked up the pace, waving.

"Wally," her dad called, pumping a man's hand and slapping him on the back.

And before Taylor knew it, they were in a crowd of people. As the grown-ups jabbered, Taylor looked at the posters of bands. They were mainly older people wearing clothes from a long time ago. One guy had on tight jeans and a black leather jacket with the collar turned up. He was playing drums just like her dad's.

Taylor blinked. It *was* her dad.

And was the woman with the microphone to her mouth . . . the woman wearing a red-and-white polka-dot skirt belted in really tight at the waist . . . *her mother*?

Taylor practically pressed her nose to the glass. It *was* her mother.

"And this must be your daughter," a woman was saying, handing Taylor's mother some papers to sign.

Taylor's mom nodded.

The woman grappled a purple hoop big enough for a dog to jump through out of a stack of other hoops and handed it to Taylor.

"Watch this!" said a girl a few feet away. She hung her red hoop around her waist and begin to gyrate like crazy. Taylor could see her moving her lips as she counted. Seventeen, so far.

"You do it too!" she commanded Taylor, not losing count.

Taylor tried, but on the fifth spin, the hoop

wobbled down her legs and bounced on the floor.

The girl let hers fall, hooked it with her foot, and flipped it into her hand.

"You're really good," Taylor said. The girl was wearing a crown. A very sparkly diamond crown— though the diamonds probably weren't real. "Are you like the queen of hula hooping or something?"

"Nope." The girl smiled, showing dimples. "I'm the Queen of the Hop."

What was that?

"Come on, Diana," a man called. "We need to get unpacked and settled in."

"See you," the girl called over her shoulder as her family headed across the lobby to the elevators.

The woman behind the registration desk was still handing out folders and plastic bags full of stuff. "You'll need your name tag too," she told Taylor. "It'll get you into all the events. And I see you're one of our rock-and-roll babies!" She handed Taylor a big glitter pink star with PEGGY SUE written in gold. "We have two Dianas, a Donna, and a Susie coming this year."

Taylor looked at her dad. He winked.

Surely he knew her real name, didn't he? But she didn't want to make a fuss, so she put on the gaudy name tag.

On the way up in the elevator, Taylor watched as downtown Reno and then the desert and mountains fell away below her, until her stomach nearly came out her mouth. She turned around, pretending to read the bulletin board. Right in front of her face was the schedule of youth events. At four o'clock, there would be a hula hoop contest.

Her mother put her hand on Taylor's shoulder. "I don't like these elevators either," she said.

They got off on the thirty-eighth floor. Taylor's head felt tight, like it might pop. Isn't that what happened to balloons when they drifted up too high? They popped?

Her mother put the key card in the door. When it opened, Taylor saw a big room with a couch and chairs, and even a table for eating. There was a tiny kitchen. They were so high up, she thought she might be able to see home from the floor-to-ceiling windows.

"Look, Taylor," her mother said, leading the way. "You've got your own bedroom and closet and bathroom and everything."

Her bedroom had floor-to-ceiling windows too, and mirrors on the opposite wall that reflected nothing but the cloudless sky. It was like floating in space.

Taylor flopped onto her bed, burying her face in the pillows.

"You okay?" her mom asked.

Taylor nodded.

"Alrighty then. I'm going to change my shirt and get back down to rehearsal. You'll probably want to eat before your dad and I are back."

She gave Taylor a quick lesson in ordering room service. "We'll be in the Painted Desert Room, and I'll have my cell phone on." She got it out of her purse and turned it on. Taylor noticed she didn't check voice mail—just slid the phone in her jeans pocket.

"Is yours on?"

Taylor took it out of her backpack and looked. It

felt weird to have her own phone. She didn't even know her phone number.

"So we're connected at all times," her mother said.

She went into her bedroom and shortly came out wearing a different shirt and a fresh coat of lipstick. "See you in a couple of hours. Call me if you get scared or worried. Watch a movie. When your dad and I get back we'll make microwave popcorn, okay?"

"Okay."

"Make sure the door is double locked after I leave." She showed Taylor how to do that. "Don't let anybody in except room service. And look through the peephole first."

Taylor listened to her mother's footsteps fade into silence. As she turned to look out across the desert, she felt the tower sway. Suddenly she longed for the feel of grass beneath her feet, and earth that seemed to give a little when you curled your toes against it.

Chapter 19

TAD WOKE UP IN A PANIC. His diggers scrabbled against something slick and hard. Rain much colder than any he'd ever felt before was thundering down on his back. Human hands tossed and tumbled him with the carrots. He felt the dirt he'd slept in being rinsed away from soft parts between his legs and belly, from the cracks between his diggers, from the crevices around his eyes.

As he was lifted, dripping, with a batch of carrots and lettuce, shaken three times, and put down on a board, Tad stared up at an enormous sky of many glaring white suns.

The board began to jiggle as a sharp thing came flying down. *Chop! Chop! Chop! Chop! Chop!*

Bits of carrots exploded around Tad like the end of the world. *Chop! Chop! Chop!*

He leaped under the ruffle of a large leaf of lettuce. And there, like a gift, was a little gray slug. Even in his terror, Tad's tongue snapped out. It was a one-blink bite.

He backed farther into the lettuce as human voices called to one another and the sharp thing sliced and diced all around him.

A hand plopped down on a cucumber that was

twice as big as Tad and, right in front of his eyes, hacked it into slices. Tad nearly fainted.

Then radishes were diced with dazzling speed, always the sharp thing going, going, going.

Tad tried to stay still, to be as small and lettucey-looking as he could possibly be. His terror wouldn't let him think.

Everything moved so fast. Some pieces of fruit fell on his head. Fingers tossed them all together, Tad being tumbled with everything else, upside down and right side up, until he thought he was going to be sick. Then he was scooped up with lettuce, carrots, cucumber, radishes, and fruit, and dropped in a bowl. He took cover again under a crispy leaf.

Peeking out, Tad saw a few acornlike things rain down from above, and then everything went dark.

Chapter 20

TAYLOR PUT DOWN THE PHONE after talking to room service. She'd ordered a pepperoni pizza and a garden salad to be sent to room 3810. She'd never talked to room service before. She'd tried to make her voice sound grown-up and not shake even a little bit.

She sat on her bed hugging her knees, wishing she could talk to her grandmother. But her grandmother was in the hospital trying to get her strength back, and Taylor didn't want to bother her. She imagined Eve's house growing dark as the sun went down. Empty and quiet. If Taylor could magically transport herself home, what would she see? Had the awful thing already happened?

She wandered through the silent suite. It was so strange being all alone. She wasn't exactly scared. She knew she could call her mom.

The sun was starting to go down, and the desert sky was pretty shades of purple, pink, and blue. Although it was still plenty light, Taylor turned on the lamps.

She drifted into her parents' bedroom. Her mother had laid out their rock-and-roll clothes. Taylor stepped into the black flats, the ones her mom was wearing in the picture on the poster. She did a few steps of the rocking kind of dance her mom had done with her dad, then she put the shoes back where she'd found them.

She cinched a wide belt over her jeans and shirt. It was too big on her.

When a knock sounded on the door and a voice called, "Room service!" Taylor whisked off the belt.

The room service person put a tray on the table between the couch and the TV. Taylor picked off a crispy curl of pepperoni and sucked on it, then

poked around in her salad looking for things she liked. She'd ordered the salad mainly because the description on the menu made her think of all the things she and her grandmother had planted.

Taylor saw it a split second before it moved.

She screamed, leaping back, banging her leg on the coffee table. The toad bounced right into the middle of her pizza, then hopped again, brushing the can of a soft drink. It scrabbled against the damp napkin, trying to get off the tray.

What was a toad doing in her salad?

Man, it had scared her.

"It's okay," she said, her voice shaking. "It's okay, little guy."

It froze, its mouth pressed to the edge of the tray. Taylor could see its heartbeat through the thin papery-looking skin.

Her heart was pounding too. What should she do?

148

Should she call room service? But what would *they* do? You never knew about people. Sometimes they were mean to small animals.

Should she call her mother? But her parents were in the middle of a rehearsal. They wouldn't want to deal with a toad crisis.

She didn't want it hopping around getting stepped on or lost under the furniture. It could get hurt wandering around a hotel.

She'd seen a little park with a fountain a couple of blocks away as they drove in. She could take him there. He would have water and could catch bugs.

But should she leave the hotel by herself?

Her mother had said not to let anybody in but room service. But she hadn't actually said not to leave the room. And it would just take her a minute. She'd be back before her parents even knew she was gone.

Taylor went into the bathroom and got a washcloth and dampened it, hoping she was doing the right thing. When she came back, the toad had turned around the other way. "Now, it's going to be all right," she said. "Don't you worry."

When her shaking hand clamped around him, she felt him scrambling, his feet in the air, struggling so much she almost dropped him.

"Not to worry," she crooned, shaking almost as much as he was. She wrapped him in the moist cloth, trying not to squish him, and gently deposited him in her backpack.

"We'll just take a little walk," she said, making sure she had her key card before she left the room.

It was spooky in the vast corridor of the hotel all alone, waiting forever for the elevator, staring out at the dusk, and watching the city of Reno rise up to meet her. The elevator stopped with a bounce that made her stomach bounce too.

In the enormous lobby, there were doors on all four sides. From far away, Taylor thought she could hear the music from her parents' rehearsal. She stood in the middle of the lobby, turning around to study each door. Which one had they come in earlier? That would be the way to the park.

"Oooops," somebody said, crashing into her. "Sorry."

"That's okay," she said, but the woman was already gone.

Although the lobby was jam-packed, Taylor had never felt so alone.

Chapter 21

TAD CROUCHED IN TERRIFIED STILLNESS. He had been picked up by a human and put in some kind of dark nest! And now he was swaying along bumpity-bump. He rose up on his diggers and peered out of an opening. The music he'd heard in his winter dreams thudded somewhere far away, and he felt a wisp of hope. Was it possible, in spite of everything that had gone wrong, that he had somehow gotten to the right place?

He saw humans, more humans than he had ever imagined. And, most amazing, he saw a flat toad drifting in the air, only this toad was as big as a human. He saw another one! And another one!

They were flying through the air everywhere.

Then he got turned a different way and he saw . . . could it be? Only a few hops away. The queen!

"Oh kiss me, moonbeams!" he cried. It was truly the queen. As Seer had promised, she wore the special shapes that marked her as the human he was to kiss. She was dark on top, like a crow, and she *was looking right at him.* "Queen!" he cried. "Over here! Over here!"

She waved.

He waved back. "Quick!"

She came close as if knowing what was supposed

to happen. She was so near. She bent down, her face only inches from his, looking at him with dark eyes. She said something he didn't understand. She was only a tongue flick away.

Moondoggies!

He tried not to think about what would happen. He thought only of home and the pond. Of Seer and his friends.

He took aim.

Then the nest jerked and he tumbled to the bottom. By the time he scrambled back to the opening, the queen was gone.

Nooooo! He had to get back to her. He dug and scrambled, hopped and lurched, trying to break free.

But he just swayed out into the night air, getting farther and farther from her every second.

He watched through the opening, trying to mark the path he was taking so he could find his way back when he got out of the nest. But soon all the shapes and lights became blurs, in spite of his efforts to keep them straight. He was in a humanville without end, coverings everywhere. He saw none of the markers that he usually used to find his way around. No iris spear chewed off at the top by a rabbit. No interesting stones half buried in the grass. No sandy path pointing the way up Cold Bottom Road.

He was terrified—though he had to admit that the gentle, rocking rhythm as the human carried him along in the nest didn't feel scary. But she was taking him away from where he needed to be.

Soon he heard a sound like hard rain on the pond back home. The rocking stopped, and Tad was set down with a bump.

Human hands lifted him out into the warm night air.

He had never seen anything like it. Enormous lit-up shapes loomed over him. Lights pulsed and chased each other. Beams of color moved like blowing tree branches.

Tad was deposited, gently, on the edge of a gigantic spewing pond. Water shot up into the sky until it touched the stars. And when it splashed back down, the drops of moisture felt wonderful on his back.

He sat frozen, trying to imagine he was the color of the covering on which he sat. He hoped he was becoming invisible.

But the human was talking, and she seemed to be talking to him. Her face was close to his, as the queen's had been, and Tad saw himself reflected in her pale eyes. What could she be saying?

He thought maybe she was encouraging him to do something. But what? Not get in the spewing pond, he hoped. He was a garden toad, not a water frog.

A cricket sang nearby. He was very hungry. But he'd have to get in the grass to catch the cricket, and he'd have to move to get in the grass, and he was too terrified to move.

He felt the girl's fingers closing around him. He tried to escape, but it was too late.

She put him in the grass and kept on talking. Did she want him to eat a cricket?

Tad's tongue flicked out. The cricket had a strange taste, but it made him feel stronger. He hopped through the grass. He found three Japanese beetles and four mosquitoes. And the next time he noticed, he was alone. The human had left.

She had been a kind human, taking him to food and water. But where in creation was he? He turned in a circle, looking at the bright shapes piercing the pale, tired-looking stars.

He had to get back to the place of flying toads, the place of the music. He had to get back to the queen. And so he began. One hop, and then another.

And another.

And another.

And another.

Chapter 22

TAYLOR WALKED BACK TOWARD THE HOTEL. She hadn't realized how far she'd come in her quest for just the right place to leave the little toad. The giant white H of their hotel against the skyline didn't look very far off, but Taylor was shocked at how long it took to get back.

Car horns were honking and the sidewalks were crowded. A mob of people turned and rushed like a school of fish toward a limo pulling up at the curb, and a woman wearing enough sparkly jewelry to light up the night stepped out of the car and made her way into a hotel. On the next block, teenagers drove a noisy black car with a pink fender up on the sidewalk and began unloading musical instruments.

Two couples pushing strollers, one with twins, took up most of the sidewalk. As they waited for the light to change, one of the women looked at Taylor, seeming to wonder what a child was doing roaming around alone. Traffic roared past. When the light turned green, Taylor rushed ahead. When she spotted another family, she sort of tagged along, hanging a little behind, trying to look like she belonged.

What was that noise? She'd been hearing it off and on since she'd left the hotel. And then she realized it was coming from her. From her backpack. She dropped her backpack right in the middle of the sidewalk and dug around for her phone. People went around her like a river parting for a rock.

FOUR MISSED CALLS

"Hello?" she said, knowing she was in big trouble.

"Oh, baby, are you all right? Where are you?" Her mother was half sobbing and half screaming.

"I'm fine," Taylor rushed to explain. "Really, I am."

"Where are you?"

Taylor looked around. How could she describe exactly where she was?

"I'm in front of the banner that says World Ecology Conference." Then she realized there were many of these banners lining the streets, all with the logo of a toad.

"Where is that?" her mother asked, her voice shrill.

"I don't know, but I can see our hotel. It's kind of just across the street."

"Oh, thank God." Taylor could hear her mother sniffling and saying something to her dad. "What are you doing there? Are you alone? Are you *sure* you're okay? We thought you'd disappeared off the face of the earth. We tried to call you just to make sure you were okay and you didn't answer and so we came to the room and you weren't here!"

"Well, I'm okay." If she tried to explain about the toad in her salad, it would sound so strange. Her parents weren't into things like toads. They wouldn't understand why she had to find a really good spot for him. "I just wanted to walk around a little bit."

More murmuring between her parents.

"Can you see the front entrance of the hotel?" her dad asked, taking the phone. Taylor didn't like the strangled sound in his voice.

She nodded. Maybe her parents did notice her after all.

"Peggy Sue?"

Tears stung her eyes. She'd really scared them.

"I can see the front entrance," she said. "Really, Dad, I'm okay. I'm sorry I made you worry."

He made a strange sound. "Okay. We're going to stay on the phone. You walk toward the front entrance, and you should see me coming out soon. When you do, wave great big."

When they caught sight of each other, Taylor began to run toward her dad. He put his arms around her shoulders and drew her against his side. "Why did you do such a thing?" he said, holding her back. "You terrified us. Oh, baby. What would we do if we lost you?"

Taylor's throat ached. Honestly, she'd always thought her parents didn't pay the least attention to her. She took a deep breath. "Well . . ."

"And you've got your backpack!" her dad exclaimed. He turned her to face him and squatted down to eye level. "Were you *running away*?" His face was white in the weird city-night lights.

She shook her head. "Of course I wasn't running away." She pulled her backpack open. "Look, it's empty. If I were running away, it would be full."

"Then why are you carrying it?"

"Well . . ." She took another deep breath. "See, I ordered room service like you said I could. And a toad jumped out of the salad bowl." She cut a look at her dad. Was he following it so far? "And I had to find a good place to put him, so I carried him in my backpack to a fountain way over that way." Taylor pointed generally in the direction of the satisfactory spot she'd found for the little toad.

Her dad gazed at her, his mouth open a little, then he shut it. "Taylor, you don't need to lie to me," he said quietly.

She swallowed. It wasn't a lie. But she didn't feel like talking about it anymore. "I'm sorry," she whispered. She saw the hurt look on her dad's face.

"Okay," he said with a sigh. "Let's just go home."

When they got back to the suite, Taylor felt her mother's face still damp with tears as they hugged, and her mother asked her why she'd left the room. Her dad cleared his throat and coughed. "Well, look," her mother said, dropping the subject, "you didn't even eat your pizza. We could heat it in the microwave."

She hadn't eaten since lunch, but she really couldn't eat a pizza a toad had hopped in. She didn't want to bring up the toad again, though, so she just said she wasn't hungry.

Later, after she was showered and in her pajamas and in bed, her mother came in. Taylor had been hearing her mother's voice talking to somebody. Maybe to her dad. Maybe on the phone to her grandmother. She wished she were with her grandmother. She tried to hold back tears.

Her mother came into her room fluffing a pillow.

"What would you think if I slept in here with you tonight?" she asked gaily, as if it were the highlight of their trip.

"Okay." Taylor put her head under the sheets and wiped her face.

"Good," her mother said. "And tomorrow we're going to get you involved in some kids' activities."

Her mother shifted and squirmed, getting settled. Her rustling made Taylor think of the sounds of birds bedding down in the trees at home.

She wished she were sitting on her grandmother's deck right now in the darkness. The tree frogs would be singing, and she could tell her grandmother about the funny little toad. Eve would understand.

It was weird having her mother in bed with her. Taylor tried to lie still and not sniffle.

Chapter 23

AFTER THE GIRL LEFT HIM ALONE IN THE GRASS, Tad hopped madly in all directions, looking for a praying mantis to point the way back to the queen. He hopped until his legs nearly fell off. But no matter which way he went, he just hit a stream of roaring stinky things. Remembering what had happened to Buuurk, Tad felt his diggers go weak.

Worn out, he finally crouched in the night shadows and gazed at the Toad-in-the-Moon. He asked the Toad-in-the-Moon if Tumbledown was still there. He didn't expect an answer, but the silence made him sad.

Morning brought a huge thirsty sun that dried

Tad out so much he almost blew away. He barely made it back to the spewing pond in time. He snuggled his rear end into dirt that didn't feel clean, and tried to stay as cool as he could until the sun went away. With coolness he could find his way back to the queen.

He waited in his hole with his eyes and mouth showing so he could zap anything edible that happened by, but he was so twitchy with impatience that he didn't catch much.

Tad kept an eye out for the nice girl. Why had she brought him here? Maybe she was going to come back and get him and return him to the queen.

He waited and watched for the girl for a long time.

When the air was cooler and the Toad-in-the-Moon once again climbed the sky, Tad left his hole. And just on the other side of a stone he spied a small mantis. Thank the green grass! At last!

The mantis swung his arm.

Tad lined himself up in the direction the mantis pointed. He wasn't sure, but he thought it was the direction he'd come from before with the nice girl.

He set off, snapping out his tongue for several fluffy white moths.

As he knew he would, he came to the river of roaring stinky things. The minute he hopped onto the rough covering—which he simply hated doing—human feet thudded and scraped around him. He had to hop like crazy to keep from getting squashed. A foot loomed over his head, and Tad sprang away. He landed on something hard and smooth . . .

. . . and *whoa!* A breeze brushed his back as he whizzed along.

He sped in front of the roaring stinky things, who stared at him with bright eyes. Right over Tad's head was a small human foot, pink and bare, so close Tad could have flicked out his tongue and touched it.

Whatever was carrying him and the little human seemed to be moving in the direction the mantis had pointed. Thank the green grass! There were the huge white tree trunks straight ahead.

Chapter 24

TAYLOR AND HER MOTHER stood in front of the table with a KIDS' ACTIVITIES sign over it.

Taylor looked at some flyers, trying to keep her mind off what today was. It was the city council meeting, and instead of being on TV she was signing up for dumb stuff.

"Look, Taylor," her mother said. "You could go on a day trip to the planetarium and science center."

"Ummm," Taylor said. She kind of liked having her mother pay so much attention to her, but she didn't want to go to a planetarium and science center. It sounded very boring.

Diana, the girl Taylor had showed the toad to in

the lobby last night, stood by a DANCE CONTEST sign. "You should sign up for this," she said. "It's lots of fun. I won last year, as you can see." She grinned, touching her crown. "Did you take your toad to the park?"

Taylor felt her mother snap to attention beside her.

"He was *sooo* cute," Diana said.

"Where did *you* see him?" Taylor's mother asked like she was cross-examining a witness.

"In Peggy Sue's backpack when she came through the lobby."

"See?" Taylor said, looking at her mother.

Diana was saying, "—all year I've been Queen of the Hop. And this year I'll turn over my crown to the next queen. Plus, this week I'll help teach new people the steps. Do you know how to do the stroll? Or the Watusi?"

Taylor shook her head.

"Well, I can teach you. Just sign up here."

Taylor's mother said, "That's an idea, honey."

Well, it sounded better than hula hoop lessons or a trip to a museum. So she wrote her name down on the list. She was Number 11. There was a boy's name across from hers.

"Oh, I know him," Diana said. "He danced last year. He's really good."

"So is there a King of the Hop?" Taylor asked.

Diana and Taylor's mother looked at her.

"Did you ever hear of a rock-and-roll song called 'King of the Hop'?" Diana giggled.

Taylor felt stupid. She didn't know anything about this stuff.

"I gotta go," Diana said. "I have to buy some souvenirs in the gift shop. See you this afternoon, if not before."

When they were partway across the lobby, Taylor's mom put her hand on her shoulder. "About that frog—"

It was a toad. But, whatever.

"I'm sorry we didn't believe you."

Taylor sighed. "Well, the salad part sounded kind of not true, I guess."

"Still, honey. You shouldn't have gone out of the hotel by yourself."

"I know."

"Look. The band has got a short rehearsal before lunch. Do you want to come along?"

"Could I spend some time in the ecology exhibit instead?" she asked. Somehow it felt like a suitable place to be when she knew the protest was going on at home without her. She could have been in front of a TV camera this very minute, telling the world about the terrible thing that was happening to her pond.

Her mother tucked a strand of Taylor's hair behind her ear. "That's okay, I guess. Your dad and I will meet up at the door to the exhibit afterward. That's where you will be the whole time, okay?"

"Okay."

"No trips for any reason, anywhere?"

Taylor nodded.

The exhibit was huge, with lots of displays and lots of people. Taylor wandered from one fascinating part to another. She could never see all of it in an hour. How weird that the foundation's logo was a warty little toad, and a warty little toad had been on her room service tray. It made the hair on Taylor's arms kind of prickle.

"Are you interested in anything in particular?" a lady asked her.

"Toads, I guess."

"Over here." The woman led her through the crowd. "We have a whole room on toads, actually."

Inside the room, a map of the world ran around all four walls. "Toads tell us how healthy the environment is," the lady explained. "Their skins are so thin, you know. So if our air or water or soil is dirty, toads don't thrive."

Printed on the map were pictures of about a zillion kinds of toads.

"What kind of toad is that?" Taylor asked, pointing to a banner.

"Ah! That's *Bufo americanus*."

Bufo americanus. It sounded like an important toad.

"They're very people-friendly, as toads go," the woman said. "They don't mind too much if you touch them—if you touch them gently. But they're particular about their habitat."

"What do you mean?" Taylor asked.

"Well, for one thing, they need plenty of moisture. So if you plopped one of those guys down around here, for example, he'd just die. The habitat is totally

different. Here where it's dry you'd see critters like *Bufo punctatus*—or the red-spotted toad." She pointed to the map of Nevada. "Here he is. Nothing like *Bufo americanus*."

Taylor felt a pinch in her throat until she could barely speak. "Die?"

The lady looked at her oddly.

"A toad would die in the wrong habitat?" Taylor asked.

"Probably," the lady said. "They're very delicate."

"I killed him," Taylor whispered. Probably with a long, slow death of drying out in the desert.

"Killed who?" The lady's eyes flickered around the room.

"A *Bufo americanus*. I didn't mean to."

The lady looked relieved. "Well, unfortunately, honey, it happens all the time. They're so small and defenseless. They're constantly getting wiped out by lawn mowers, garden tillers, fertilizers, earthmoving equipment, traffic. I'm sure you didn't mean to."

That didn't make her feel any better. "How would a *Bufo americanus* do in Iowa?" Taylor asked.

"Oh, he'd be very happy there in somebody's nice garden, near a pond."

Taylor nodded. "Thanks," she said.

In a daze, she left the toad room. Why hadn't she just found a box for him and taken him home?

But it was too late. He was probably already dead.

She sat down on a bench outside the entrance to the ecology exhibit.

How could I have killed a toad?

Diana came out of the souvenir shop and across the atrium. "Anything interesting in there?" she asked, sitting down beside Taylor.

Taylor stared at her. "It's all pretty interesting," she said dully.

"Then I might go in and have a look. Want to go in again?"

Taylor shook her head.

"Okay. Later, then."

Alone, Taylor stared at the huge banners stirring

in the air, until a small *breeping* sound made her look down.

And there.

There.

Was her toad.

Taylor scooped him up in her hand and raced back to the amphibian room. She held the little toad up to the picture that sat right over where she lived in Iowa. He was a perfect match.

"You're coming home with me, dude," she said. "I don't care what it takes." She may have failed at everything else, but she was going to save one small toad who'd somehow gotten into the wrong habitat. "But first things first. Let's find you a box."

Chapter 25

HACK-A-MANNA! He was back in a nest! Once again, he had been practically within a tongue-flick of the queen, and then the other girl—the nice one who had taken him to the grass and water—had snatched him up and talked to big people, and everybody had jabbered on and on, and now he was in a hard-walled nest he couldn't get out of!

He dug and scraped with his diggers. He threw himself against the sides, but they pushed back, sending him tumbling across the pebbles.

Finally, Tad hunkered in the shallow water soothing his skinned places. Loneliness sat down on one side of him, and fear on the other.

Much later, the girl who had put him in the nest knelt down. She said something. And then funny little crickets rained on his head.

Tad ate them. Not because he wanted to. He had no appetite. But because his tongue came to life on its own and shot out.

The girl went away, and before long, Tad heard the bouncy music from his winter dreams. He began to rock from side to side. He'd danced to this song before. Back home. Making Buuurk laugh, then making the other toads clap and stomp. The music made him drop-dead homesick.

The girl scooped him up in her bare hands and held him near her face. Her eyes were the color of the pond on a sunny day. He saw himself in them.

He felt the music in the rocking way she moved. She put him down on the soft ground of her big room. Her feet danced around him, her toenails pink as impatiens blossoms.

As if they were being pulled by strings, Tad's diggers began to go. He found himself shaking his belly, wiggling around just a little bit. When the music went all tinkly, he moved his feet just like the girl's feet were moving. He could tell she really liked the music too. Wouldn't it be nice, he thought, if *she* were the Queen of the Hop?

Chapter 26

TAYLOR WAS PRACTICING THE WATUSI when her dad came into her room. He watched her until the song ended, and then he clapped.

"Did you learn that today?"

"Yep." Taylor was surprised at how much dancing was like running track. She had to keep her head in each moment and stay focused. And most of all, she got the same wonderful feeling after a while, as if she could fly. Her partner, Number 11, was really good, but he didn't seem happy about getting paired with her.

"You're a natural," her dad said. "Good thing we named you Peggy Sue."

Taylor laughed. "Dad, do you even know my real name?"

He gazed out the glass wall of her room at the desert sky. Then shrugged. "Bernadine?"

Taylor grabbed her balled-up socks and threw them at him.

"Thanks for helping me with the toad."

They'd found a strong box in a service alley and gone to a pet store a couple of blocks from the hotel to buy some nesting material, canned crickets, and bottled water. She never thought her parents would be interested in a toad.

"Just don't let housekeeping find him," her dad said. "There are probably rules about keeping wild animals in hotel rooms."

Yeah, he was really wild. He sat perfectly still by a chair leg—though earlier it had looked a little like he was dancing.

"Don't worry," she told her dad. "I have his box in the closet, covered with a T-shirt. Housekeeping won't see him."

"You want to call Eve?" her dad asked. "She got

home from the hospital today. Then, as soon as your mom and I have showered, we'll all go to dinner with the Mindersons. They have their kids along. Maybe we can play some miniature golf after."

"Okay, I guess. . . ." Aliens had definitely taken over her parents' bodies. Her real parents didn't play miniature golf.

After her dad was gone, she squatted down and studied the toad. "Are you a rock and roller too, dude?" she murmured, gently touching his back.

Then she called her grandmother. She told Eve about the dance competition. "I won't win. Some of the kids are really good."

"You don't know that for sure," Eve said.

"How are you feeling?"

"Pretty good." Her grandmother changed the subject. "Did you know a big world ecology conference is going on in Reno?"

"It's right here in our hotel!"

"Is it really? I was just listening to the news. John Verdun will be there. They say he's the second-richest man in the world. He gave billions and billions of dollars to a conservation group."

Taylor found it kind of hard to concentrate on what her grandmother was talking about. If the pond was gone, she wanted to know. She couldn't bear waiting. So she sat up straight, bracing herself.

"Eve, is the pond still there?"

It seemed to take forever until her grandmother said, "The pond is still here. I'm on the deck right now watching a heron."

A little sigh of relief stirred Taylor's bangs.

"How about everything else?"

"Well, while I was

in the hospital, they did some more work in the woods down by the road."

Taylor thought she had braced herself for bad news, but sadness settled in a big knot in her stomach. It was happening.

"I'm sorry," her grandmother said.

"I've gotta get ready for dinner now." Taylor didn't want to talk anymore. Not even to her grandmother. "But I'm bringing you a surprise," she said. "Something for the garden."

After she hung up, Taylor stood staring out the window. The sun was almost down. The desert and mountains faded hazily into the twilight. The little toad sat by her foot, seeming to stare out over the desert too. His jewel-like eyes turned up to hers, and he said *breep* very softly.

She squatted down by him. "Let's put some music on," she said. "It will cheer us up."

Taylor watched herself dance in the mirror of her closet door. The little toad was backlighted by the last of the hazy sunset. He almost looked like he was doing the same dance steps she was doing. And then he went off on some moves of his own.

He was *really* good. Taylor sank to the floor, staring at him in the mirror. "A desert mirage," she said out loud. "It's gotta be."

Chapter 27

WATER HAD SLOPPED OUT OF THE LITTLE POND, and Tad felt the wall of his nest softening. He began to scratch with his diggers. He worked and worked, tearing away at the stuff, pushing with his rear end to make an opening. First there was a little hole, big enough for him to stick a digger through. Then there was a bigger hole. But as the hole got bigger, the stuff got stiffer, and he felt it scraping his skin.

Finally he slid his body through and hopped toward the stars. It felt wonderful to be free. The Toad-in-the-Moon gazed back at him, and Tad felt encouraged.

He hoped to someday find his way home and

tell Seer how big Mother Earth was. He hoped home would still be there. He wished his friend Buuurk was beside him right now. *If wishes were fishes, then hop toads would fly.* That's what Seer always said. Tad would give anything to sit by Seer and ask him about the thing Tad felt growing behind his eyes. Would it keep getting bigger? When would he dream again?

The girl was sleeping nearby, her arm dangling down. As Tad hopped closer to the stars, he passed very close to her hand, which was bigger than he was. Toads were supposed to loathe being picked up by humans, so why did he never pee on her when she picked him up? Even though she kept taking him away from the queen just when he was about to kiss her?

With his face near the stars, Tad stared down at the bright, colorful lights. Some were huge blocks of brilliance that thrust up into the night sky. Some were weaving red and white snakes.

Amid all the lights and all the coverings and all the humanvilles, where were the gardens? Were there any toadvilles as far as the eye could see?

Tad turned. He had to get going.

He made his way to a crack in the girl's room that looked big enough for him to get through. Earlier, the girl had come this way when she had taken him outside. Somewhere out there was the queen.

He tried to burrow underneath, but the crack pinched him. So he threw himself forward, but he was still stuck. So he scrambled backward. Forward, backward. Forward, backward. He was getting more and more stuck and more and more flattened. In a panic, he made a desperate lunge backward and—thank the green grass!—he was unstuck.

But he was still in the girl's room and there was no other way out.

He wished he could find a way to tell her to take him to the queen. When she woke up, he'd try, somehow, to make it clear.

He climbed up to sit beside her, to wait for her awakening. She smelled nice. Actually, she smelled sort of familiar. Like borage, which was his favorite garden smell.

And she looked nice too, for a human. She was

a pretty color. Her skin was like the rose petals that the hoppers had used to soothe his painful back in Toadville-by-Birdbath. Her hair gleamed like moonlight. She didn't have any warts, though, and that was too bad.

As he sat with one of his hands resting on a strand of her hair, he imagined kissing her. He remembered when the idea of kissing a human had seemed so nasty it made him want to throw up. But now it didn't seem that bad.

It was a nice thought. A little exciting, even. He could practice the kiss on this girl.

But what would happen? Was it possible his kiss would turn her into a higher, toadly being? He would like that. He was lonely and needed a friend. But how would *she* feel? She might be afraid to change.

He sat for a long time, his hand on a soft tendril, wondering.

Chapter 28

"THIS WILL TOP THE LOOK OFF PERFECTLY," the costume lady said. She bent down and cinched a wide turquoise belt around Taylor's waist. She turned Taylor's shoulders so she was looking in the three-way mirror of the dressing room. "Waddaya think?"

Taylor tried not to roll her eyes. Great bunches of puffy pettycoat ruffles made her skirt flare out. The ruffled white top made her shoulders look bigger. And the belt made her waist look pinched in.

Taylor felt like she was turning into something else. An hourglass, maybe.

Why couldn't she just dance in her shorts and T-shirt? But her mom and dad were standing in the doorway, smiling at her in the mirror, so she guessed she could live with the look.

Actually, whatever was fastest she could live with. The little toad had gotten out of his box in the night *again*, and she had woken up to find him on her pillow *again*, tangled in her hair.

He'd dug a hole in one corner of his box. She'd put him back she didn't know how many times. If he escaped again, he might get stepped on or squashed by a housekeeping cart.

Plus, she'd dreamed rock and roll all night long and felt crabby and tired this morning as she stood waiting while her parents paid for the Peggy Sue costume.

"So did you practice last night?" Number 11 had on black trousers, white socks, and a pink shirt. Taylor wouldn't be the only one who looked silly.

"I practiced every single dance we've learned this week," she said.

"Well, let's try to win. You'll get the crown, and I'll get a fifty-dollar gift certificate."

Taylor would love to claim the sparkly crown,

even if it probably wasn't real diamonds. But she didn't think she could dance that well.

"Maybe you should ask for a different partner," she said. "It won't hurt my feelings."

"Nah," he said. "They don't let kids switch. Whoever signs up on the same line as you, you're stuck with."

"Hey, Peggy Sue." Diana rushed out of a dressing room wearing a poodle skirt.

It was hard for Taylor to remember that everybody thought her name really was Peggy Sue.

Diana twirled around, making her skirt flare out. "Isn't it over the moon? I can hardly wait." She touched her tiara. "Though it is going to be hard to give up this pretty thing."

"So what did you do during your year-long reign as Queen of the Hop?" Number 11 asked. "Work for world peace? Save the whales? Go on the *Today* show?"

Diana stuck her tongue out at him and told Taylor, "He's just jealous because he and his partner came in second last year." She turned back to Number 11. "And if you must know, when I got home I was on TV! And this lady interviewed me for a feature story in a local magazine. I wore my crown and sash and got to talk about all sorts of things."

"You were on *television*?" Taylor gasped.

"Yep. I was the 'Good News' segment one week. Ten whole minutes—except there was a cat food commercial in the middle."

Ten minutes! Taylor had worked really hard for a ten-second sound bite to save the pond. And hadn't got it.

If she won the crown, she'd probably get all kinds of interviews. And when they asked her what she wanted to accomplish during her reign, she could tell everybody about the pond. If it was still there.

She spun to Number 11. "I think we should go for it," she said. "Really try our best. We could practice together after lunch. Maybe you could help us if you wanted to," she told Diana. "Me especially."

But she had to go check on the toad first.

As she and her parents passed through the atrium, carrying Taylor's petticoats, the long banners with the toad logo fluttered gently. New posters of endangered species stood along one wall. A snout-nosed piggy-looking creature, with hair like dandelion fluff, seemed to glare at her. CHACOAN PECCARY, the label said. There was a beetle, a gecko, a soft-looking bird with a funny beak, and lots of other creatures.

Taylor would have liked to stop and look, but she didn't have time. She tugged on her dad's hand. How could grown-ups be so slow? "Hurry," Taylor said. "I need to see how the toad is doing."

Inside the suite, the housekeeper had tidied up, washed the cups in the little kitchenette, and made Taylor's bed.

Taylor opened her closet. It was empty.

The little cardboard house with water and bugs and everything, was gone. There was just a clean spot on the floor, with Taylor's T-shirt beside it.

Trembling, Taylor searched the whole suite, but her toad was gone too, of course.

It was her fault.

She shouldn't have spent so much time yakking with Diana and Number 11. She shouldn't have let her parents dawdle in the lobby.

"He's gone for good this time, isn't he?" Taylor asked, her voice cracking.

She saw the truth in the glance her parents exchanged as her dad reached out to hug her.

"Try not to feel bad, honey. You did everything you could," her mother said.

Chapter 29

THAT MORNING, AS USUAL, the girl had carried Tad to his nest as the sun came up. Her hands had smelled like the garden, and they were so soft. They had carried him just right, too. They hadn't squeezed, yet he knew she wouldn't drop him.

"Take me to the queen!" he cried as he always did, looking into her eyes. "Before it's too late!"

But she'd settled him gently back in the nest he'd escaped from the night before. Then she shook out some crickets, filled his pond, and put his nest in darkness. Like she always did.

Tad began struggling to get out once again.

He had just gotten one digger through the nest

when something roared, coming closer, going away, coming closer again. Then suddenly Tad was washed with sunlight.

Was the beast going to eat him?

It just sniffed him mightily and backed up. But a big human was staring down at Tad. She shot out something in human talk, shook her head, and raised her big ugly foot over him.

* * *

When he came to, he was in darkness, and one of his diggers throbbed with pain. Tad felt part of his nest crumpled around him, and he was being dragged along inside what seemed to be a giant sack. Some things rattled and other things crunched together, and sticky stuff dripped on his head.

He heard a *ding!* and then he was dragged a little farther. A strange feeling made his warts prickle. He was falling, even though he was sitting still. He couldn't see it, but he could feel it. Falling and falling. He had to get out!

Light came through a tiny hole in the soft, stretchy skin of the giant sack. He ripped at the hole with his good digger. When he had an opening big enough to scramble through, he tumbled out. He landed beside a human foot, the same foot that had stomped him. He was in a room that was going down, down, down until, suddenly, it stopped with a sickening bounce, and he almost lost his stale-cricket breakfast.

Ding! In front of him, two walls slid apart, and

the angry human disappeared through the opening, dragging the smelly, nasty sack that still had his nest in it. And then the walls slid back together, and the room moved downward again.

Alone, he tested his bent digger, discovering he could still hop—but barely. The room stopped with another *ding!* and the walls slid apart again, and this time he heard the special music. His music. Ignoring the pain, he lurched forward.

Wham! Bam! Thud! He scrambled to get out of the way, but feet were everywhere. Great thunders of feet. High, fast, hard feet with sharp edges. One came down on his sore digger, making stars spark around him. Another kicked him. He flew through the air, landed with a *whump!*, and slid under something.

There were no more feet in that shadowy place, but he hurt so much he knew his time of passing into the Great Cycle had surely come. Sadness covered him like the darkest night. He had failed.

Chapter 30

CAMERAS FLASHED AND FOLLOWED THE DANCERS. Taylor hung on to the waist of the boy in front of her. She hopped forward, backward, and then forward again. Even the little kids could do the bunny hop, so it was the opening dance, not competitive.

Diana sat in the front row wearing the crown and sash. When the time came, she would crown the winner.

After lunch, she'd given Taylor a bunch of tips. Listen to the music. Smile. Don't think about a single other thing. Smile. Follow your partner, but do your own stuff too. And above all *smile.*

Taylor glanced over at Diana and tried to keep a

smile on her face, though she didn't really feel like smiling. She kept thinking about the poor toad.

Ryan and the Rompers were playing for the Queen of the Hop competition. It was kind of embarrassing having her dad up in front of everybody like that, drumming the steady beat. He caught her eye and winked.

It was *really* embarrassing when her mother stepped up to the old-fashioned microphone and started to sing. But it was kind of cool too. Her mom stepped back from the microphone and gave Taylor a little wave. Taylor took her hand off the damp waist of her partner and waved back.

Her parents had stuck to her like rubber cement ever since she'd lost it over her missing toad. They'd asked housekeeping if they'd found a box in Taylor's closet, and housekeeping said they never removed boxes from guests' rooms. But Taylor was pretty sure he'd ended up in the trash compactor. She was glad she'd tried to save him. Really glad. He'd been the best toad in the world.

The bunny hop ended, and the dancers got a short

break before the competition. Taylor ran backstage for some water. Hopping around in three layers of petticoats had made her really sweaty.

They'd set up a table with pitchers of water and plates of cookies. She was gulping water when somebody cried, "Watch it!" There was a bump, a sloshing sound, then a racket as one of the plastic pitchers bounced on the floor.

Kids leaped back. The white tablecloth turned dark, as water soaked through it and dripped off. The puddle spread under the table.

It was briefly very quiet as everybody put on an *I didn't do it!* look, and backed away. Taylor could hear the emcee out front explaining to the audience how the elimination would work.

Then backstage, the racket started up again. Number 11 handed Taylor a sign, which she hung around her neck.

"We gonna shake it?" he asked, doing a wiggly thing that made Taylor laugh.

Taylor crammed a cookie in her mouth and nodded. "Shake it," she mumbled around the crumbs.

They didn't know what songs the band would play. That was the whole point. They had to show that they could dance to any of the songs. To improvise, just like they were at a real *hop* in the 1950s, which her grandmother had explained was a dance event back in the day when kids had to take off their shoes to dance on the gym floor. That's why they'd been called *sock hops*.

Taylor would be glad to take off her shoes. They were already pinching. And she was relieved that the first song, "Smoke Gets in Your Eyes," was slow and smooth, because water was still sloshing around in her stomach.

Tad was in a little puddle of water.

Water.

He sat in the water, waiting a long time, until it finally began to fluff him up. The shadowy form of the Great Cycle rolled away, and Tad heard the music. A roach carrying a cookie crumb strolled past and—*zot!*—was inside Tad in the blink of an eye.

206

After a while, Tad tried to hop. He hurt all over, especially one of his diggers. But he could move.

Taylor caught her dad's eye as Number 11 twirled her around. Her skirt spun like a Frisbee, and she was flying. Number 11 pulled her back and they touched palms, pushing away from each other. She smiled.

The band was on
the second song, and
the judges were starting
to make their way
through the couples to
cut in as they called it,
though it really meant,
Sit down, you're finished.

Taylor knew that could happen to her and Number 11 any second. But she kept her mind on the music. Nothing else.

By the time the band started the fifth song, there were only seven couples left. The dancers had done the shag and the stroll and the Watusi. She had a hard time holding on to Number 11's hands because they were so sweaty. But she felt *good.*

When it got down to three couples, Taylor was totally into the music. But then her feet slid out from under her and she was on her butt.

She stared at Number 11's knees.

The drums missed a beat, and she felt a million eyes on her.

Number 11 swung his leg over her head, grabbed her hand, and spun her around on the floor. She jumped up, and Number 11 made a little bow like they'd been practicing that special move all week.

Taylor bowed too. But mainly she smiled.

The audience clapped and her dad drummed louder.

Still. Taylor was sure the judges knew she'd fallen.

Finally, only two couples were left on the floor. This was it. Number 11 squeezed her hand.

"Fifty dollars," he whispered.

"The crown," she whispered back.

It would be fine to be interviewed on TV and in the newspaper and be able to talk about the pond—if it was still there when she got home. But whatever happened, she was having fun. She wiped the sweat off her face and wiped her hands on her blouse.

The last song, as everybody knew, would be "Queen of the Hop."

"Smile," she whispered to Number 11.

As her mother's voice trailed off into softness for

the last words of the song, one of the judges said something to Diana.

The audience applauded as the two couples joined hands and bowed. A trickle of sweat shot down the side of Taylor's cheek as she bent forward. It stopped at the corner of her mouth, and she licked it away.

The room went silent. Taylor's heart was practically flinging her into the air. Diana stood up. She looked at both couples as she came onto the stage. She removed the crown from her head and placed it on Taylor's. The audience went crazy clapping as one of the judges draped the sash over Taylor's shoulder.

The crown felt wobbly on her head. She held it with one hand and told the other girl how well she'd danced, and better luck next year. Then she kissed Number 11 on the cheek and waved at everybody.

All the dancers came back for one last song. The band broke into "Peggy Sue." She felt so happy that Peggy Sue was sort of her name that tears came to her eyes.

Tad tried to understand what he was seeing. There was *his* girl—the one he liked more than night-smacky-goo—wearing the special shapes that marked her as the queen.

"Oh, kiss me, moonbeams!" he cried, finally believing his eyes. "Moondoggies!"

He forgot he hurt. He forgot everything except what he was going to do next. He was going to kiss the Queen of the Hop. He wiggled and bounced, shaking his belly. He even did a flip.

Taylor was desperate for a drink. But what was that on the floor, right at the edge of the stage?

It was her toad! He hadn't been squashed in the trash compactor!

Taylor dropped Number 11's hand and ran to save the little guy before kids stampeded backstage.

"I'm so glad to see you, toad!" She scooped him up and ran behind the curtain. Where could she put him that would be safe for a few minutes? "I am so *very* glad to see you," she whispered, holding him close to her face.

His eyes glistened. He looked tired but proud. "Oh, you are *soooo* cute!" And she gave him a great big kiss.

Taylor's last thought before something exploded and she crumpled to the floor was, *Did I actually smooch a toad that had been hopping around on the floor???* And then darkness closed in around her.

Chapter 31

WHAT HAD HAPPENED?

It was like he'd been sucked up in a whirlwind, pulled apart, jammed back together again, and spat out on the ground. The crumbs on the floor looked tiny and far away. Everything looked different. Way different. He felt so dizzy, the roach he had just eaten swirled around in his stomach and almost came back up.

"Hey," he said to the girl, although he knew she couldn't understand him. "Are you okay?"

Her eyes fluttered opened, then closed again.

It was his girl. The Queen of the Hop. And she had kissed him; he remembered that now. She had picked him up with her soft hands that smelled like the garden and kissed him.

He'd been trying to kiss her. Something had gone terribly wrong.

The girl's eyes opened. Her eyes had always made him think of the clear water of the pond. He gazed into them, but he didn't see himself. He saw a human.

He leaped back. *Hack-a-manna!*

He was as big as she was! Bigger. *Where were his fine warts?* His rear diggers? What had happened to him??

"What happened?" his girl murmured. "Have you seen my toad?" She tried to sit up, and he helped her. Her palm felt so soft and familiar that he shivered.

His hand looked just like hers! He understood what she said.

He fought the panic that rose in him.

"My toad has got to be around here somewhere," she said. "I must have slipped on the slick floor and bumped my head and dropped him."

She stood up. He stood up too. Everything whirled like it was going to tilt him off the edge.

How could he be so enormous? How could he stand on two long, straight digger things?

He tried to flick his tongue. It didn't work.

A human came dashing up. He wore a sign around his neck that matched the girl's sign. "Come on, Taylor! People are freaking out. We're supposed to be taking bows and posing for pictures."

The girl snatched up her crown and ran, calling over her shoulder, "If you see a little toad, take care of him until I get back, okay? Don't let him get away! He's really special." Then she disappeared in the direction the music was coming from.

Tad was soon surrounded by humans who paid no attention to him, though he felt as freakish as a seven-legged cricket. He had on clothes, he realized. And on the front of his belly was a picture of a toad that made his heart hammer with homesickness.

He felt dried out and longed to squat down in the puddle of water, but it was so small. He watched the humans move water from one place to another, then put it in their mouths. When nobody was watching, he tried it.

216

It would have been a lot easier just to sit in the puddle, but he felt refreshed after he did it the human way. He did it over and over.

"Dude, save some for the rest of us!" a human said.

Tad was so hungry, he could have eaten a mulch pile of earthworms. A roach darted out, but was gone again before Tad could even move. He looked around. He didn't see any more, but it was hard to spot bugs from this high up. That's it, he thought; he was going to starve.

Chapter 32

TAYLOR HELD NUMBER 11'S HAND and made one last bow. She'd done it. *They'd* done it.

She felt like punching the air and screaming *Yes!* But that would be a little bit rude. She really hoped the pond would still be there when she got home so she could talk about it on TV.

She squeezed Number 11's hand before she turned him loose. "You just won fifty dollars," she whispered.

He grinned. "You look good in that crown. And you ended up being a really good partner. Nice recovery when you fell on your butt."

She shrugged. "Sometimes things don't work out like you plan." She felt very grown-up and wise. She must have breathed too much oxygen.

She and Diana's flashed each other a thumbs-up.

The second-place winner looked mopey backstage, so Taylor said, "I'll bet you take home the crown next year."

And then it occurred to Taylor that she would *have* to come back next summer to crown the new queen.

Backstage, everybody was putting on their street shoes and grabbing the last of the cookies. Taylor had to find her toad. She could hardly believe he had somehow escaped the trash compacter.

"Hey, want to go get some ice cream with me and my parents?" Number 11 asked. "To celebrate?" He grinned. "I'll buy."

"I can't," Taylor said. "I've got to find a toad."

"What do you need with a toad?" Then he slapped his legs. "Oh, right! I get it. You're the Queen of the *Hop.*"

Taylor gave him a look. "I've got to find *my* toad. I had him just a few minutes ago."

Number 11 took a step back. "Okay," he said. "Catch you later, then."

Down the alley made by the stage curtains, Taylor could see Ryan and the Rompers packing up their instruments. Her parents would be coming to claim her soon.

Then she caught sight of the boy in the T-shirt with the toad on the front. "Hey," she called. "Have you seen my toad?"

He looked at her strangely. What was wrong with boys? Didn't they know girls could like toads too?

"Seriously," she said. "He's in the wrong habitat here. I've got to find him and take him home to my grandmother's garden."

"Toads are small," the boy said. "*Really* small."

Well, *duh*. "This little guy was so small he hid in

my salad the first night we were here. I've had an awful time hanging on to him."

She glanced back at the stage. The band was almost packed. "Will you help me look?"

"Okay."

She checked under the table. That would be a good place for him. Out of the way of feet and where there was water. But no, he wasn't there. She looked under the edge of the stage curtain.

The boy in the T-shirt seemed to be kind of copying her. Making the same moves she did. It was a little annoying.

"What's going on?" her dad said, coming backstage.

"Did you see my toad?" Taylor asked.

"Oh, honey." Her mother was tidying up her ponytail. "I thought we'd decided he ended up in the trash compactor."

"But he *didn't*! He somehow turned up backstage during the dance. I swear. I saw him."

Her parents glanced at each other.

"He's still here," the boy said.

He said it like he had X-ray vision or something.

"Well, *where*?"

"Let's look," her dad said. "If all four of us look, it shouldn't take long. And I hope not, because, I've gotta tell you, I'm hungry."

The boy's stomach growled so loud Taylor almost laughed.

After they'd lifted up everything and looked in all the shadows backstage, and hunted among the seats, they still hadn't found him. As they searched, the boy kept banging into things. He was very clumsy.

"Honey, I'm starting to think that toad can take care of himself," her mother said. "Maybe he got another ride back to Iowa."

"No, he didn't," the boy said. "He's still here."

Why did he keep saying that? It was almost like he knew more about her toad than she did.

"Well, he seems to have at least nine lives," Taylor's dad said. "Let's go get pizza. Maybe he'll turn up."

"But—"

The boy's stomach rumbled and gurgled. He put his hand over it and looked embarrassed. "Don't worry about the toad. He'll be okay."

Well, fine. She hoped he knew what he was talking about.

The boy rode down in the elevator with them. He stared at the colored lights on the panel like he had never seen such a thing. When they got out in the atrium, Taylor's dad said, "Is your family here?"

"Yes!" the boy said so loudly that a couple of people turned.

He was dorky, but kind of cute.

"What's your name?" Taylor asked him. "I'm—" She didn't want to say *Taylor*, for a change. "Peggy Sue."

"My name's Tad. You're a great dancer."

Taylor touched her tiara. Yes, she was. "Thanks. I

just learned this week. Do you dance?"

The boy seemed thoughtful. Not like some boys who just shoved you in the lunchroom line and said smarty things.

Tad nodded. "I love that music."

Taylor was surprised. Most kids thought old rock and roll was kind of silly. Just like she used to.

"You want to eat with us?" she asked.

"Yes!" he said, startling a lady in front of them who turned around to sneak a peek.

She stopped her parents. "Dad, can Tad eat with us?"

"If his family says it's okay."

"Why don't you ask your family?" Taylor said.

He walked over to where some people were gathered outside the amphibian room. He stumbled over his own feet a couple of times before he disappeared inside. When he came out, he said, "It's okay."

As they walked to the pizza place, they passed the fountain where Taylor had taken the little toad that first night. She was so hot, and the water looked so sparkly and cool. "I'd like to just sit down and let the water splash on me," she said.

"Me too!"

Taylor laughed. Why did he seem so familiar? And why did he walk in the grass like he was allergic to concrete?

Chapter 33

"SO ARE YOU AND YOUR FAMILY really into saving the toads?" the queen's mom asked Tad as someone set down their food.

"That's why I'm here."

The delicious-smelling stuff put in front of him made him think of big ladybugs. But he couldn't zot because he no longer had a fine toadly tongue.

He watched how the queen ate. She picked up the leaf-shaped thing that the ladybug-like things sat on. And she used her teeth to crunch them into pieces. He practiced clicking his own teeth together.

When she saw him watching her, she turned a pretty pink. And magically it made him feel like he was turning pink too.

"What?" she said.

"Nothing."

He picked up the water. He'd like to just dump it over his head, but he held it up to his mouth like the humans did. And he used the hard things in his mouth to take a piece of the food and eat it. It tasted strange . . . but okay.

"Isn't this the best?" the queen asked him.

"Oh yeah!" he said. "It makes me think of ladybugs."

Her crown was a little crooked. He fixed it.

"My grandmother has a garden with ladybugs in it," she said.

"She does? Gardens are great. Dirt, mulch, ponds, bugs, worms. Gardens are . . . awesome!"

The girl sat beside him smiling, her face all sunshiny.

He remembered sitting on a rock with Buuurk,

waiting for the first queen. And he remembered sitting on a rock with Seer, owning up to his dreams. He'd give anything to talk to Seer or Buuurk again, to be a toad again, to sit by Father Pond.

"So where are you from, Tad?" the queen's mom asked.

"Toadville-by-Tumbledown." His heart was squeezed with longing.

"What a quaint name. It sounds absolutely charming."

"What does your dad do?" the queen's dad asked.

How could he answer that question? If he said he was really a toad, and toads didn't exactly have moms and dads, they'd think he was crazy. Seer was kind of like a dad, though, so he said, "My dad has dreams."

"Ah, a visionary," the queen's mom said. "I expect the ecology movement needs a few of those."

Tad hoped *he* might have a vision. And soon. He desperately needed to know how to get out of this mess he was in. He rubbed the place between his eyes. His skin was warm. And so much thicker. He rubbed the top of his head. He was furry, like the humans.

The girl's hand was on the bench beside his. He used to be smaller than her hand. How could he be so positively, enormously *huge*? He had to get out of this clumsy human body. He would terrify all the toads at home. They'd never recognize him. And more than anything else, he wanted to go home.

Chapter 34

"LET'S WALK THROUGH the ecology exhibit," Taylor said as they entered the hotel atrium. "I'll pick up some stuff for my grandmother."

The huge banners with the toad logo rippled slowly. The boy was gazing at them in the way that Taylor sometimes saw her grandmother gazing at a perfect ruffled poppy or an amazing sky.

"I could use a nap," her dad said.

Her mother sighed. "I'm tired too, honey. Let's look later. Maybe before the closing banquet tonight."

"But this ends for good in a couple of hours." Taylor pointed to a sign.

"Oh," Taylor's mother said. "I didn't realize they'd

be taking things down today. We'd better look while we can, I guess."

Her parents drifted off to a model of a rain forest.

"Where's your family?" Taylor asked Tad.

His eyes scanned the huge atrium. "Over there," he said, pointing to the amphibian exhibit.

"That's where I found out my toad was in the wrong habitat. He's *Bufo americanus*. I don't know where he came from or how he got here, but I need to take him home."

"Don't worry," Tad said. "He's around."

Why was he so sure?

Taylor caught a glimpse of herself reflected in a huge poster of the large-billed reed warbler. She'd forgotten all about her Queen of the Hop regalia. She probably looked kind of silly. She could take off the sash and crown, but then what would she do with them? But her dance shoes were setting her feet on fire every time she moved. She stepped out of them and felt much better. Carrying them, she followed Tad down the row of large photographs.

A lady was explaining, "These are all creatures

that environmentalists thought had died out long ago, but have been rediscovered. It's very exciting to know there are a few still with us. But if we're not careful with the environment, they'll certainly be wiped out forever."

"Holy tadpoles, look at that," Tad said, leading the way to a photograph of a brown fish about the size of two men.

"'Coelacanth,'" Taylor read. It was pronounced *see*-luh-canth, according to the sign. The fish was thought to have been extinct for more than sixty-five million years until one was found off the coast of South Africa in 1938.

"I'd hate to meet one of those in the pond," Tad said.

It was huge and hideously ugly. "It reminds me of my mud puppy," Taylor told him. "I made this papier-mâché mud puppy for my class's unit on amphibians. Have you ever seen a mud puppy?"

Tad shook his head.

"Me neither, but I'd like to someday. Oh, look at

this," she said, moving on to the next photograph. "This guy is cute."

A furry critter with a pink nose and big eyes clung to a stem of bamboo. He was described as a Monito del Monte, a small marsupial believed to have been extinct for eleven million years until one was discovered in a thicket of bamboo somewhere in Chile.

Taylor peered at her reflection in the glass. What was that on her chin? Pizza sauce? Why hadn't somebody told her she had food on her face? She turned away and wiped it off, hot with embarrassment.

When she looked at Tad again, he was staring at her bare feet. Why? She put one behind the other, trying to hide them. But it didn't work. She just ended up walking backward.

"I like that shiny pink stuff on your toes," Tad said.

Taylor felt her feet blush, and she put her shoes back on.

"Look!" Tad cried.

She followed to where he was pointing. It was one of the photographs at the end of the near-extinct species exhibit. He was practically leaping toward it.

"What is it?" she asked, catching up with him. It looked like a shiny pale blue beetle magnified many times. BLUE TOPAZ BEETLE, the label said. Taylor read aloud. "'Sometimes referred to as "the jewel of all beetles," the blue topaz beetle is considered one of the rarest insects in the world. Believed extinct for thousands of years, a small colony of fewer than thirty individuals was found living in rotting wood near a small pond in Minnesota.'"

"There are some where I live," Tad said.

"And where is that?" the lady coming up behind them asked.

"By Tumbledown, near the pond, in a field with flowers."

Taylor felt a surge of homesickness so great that she crossed her arms over her stomach. He could be describing *her* home.

"I live in a place just like that," she said. "There's

beautiful woods and grassy hills and the nicest pond. And an old tumbledown shed. And the terrible thing is that they're going to tear it all up and drain the pond!"

The lady sighed. "And that's exactly why the blue topaz beetle is almost extinct. We're destroying their habitat."

"But I know where there are some more!" Tad insisted. "Truly!"

The lady handed him one of the postcards with

the blue topaz beetle on its front. "Many beetles look similar to each other," she said. "It's very unlikely you've seen the particular blue topaz beetle. But if you think you really have, there's contact information on the card for reporting sightings. Lots of environmentalists would get *very excited* if you found some more."

Tad put the card in his T-shirt pocket.

As the lady walked away, Taylor studied the beetle. "It honestly does look kind of like a precious jewel," she said.

Wasn't it odd that the way he'd described his home made it sound just like hers?

Chapter 35

TAD WAITED ON A BENCH. The bench was beside a bush with soft tendrils of white flowers that smelled nice. He twisted them into a garland, remembering how he and Buuurk had made garlands for Anora and Shyly.

With his human hands he was making a very big garland. If Anora and Shyly were here this very minute, he would be able to hold both of them in his open hand.

The human world was too big. Too complicated. He didn't know how to use the picture of the beetle to talk to the people who would want to know where the beetle lived. Anyway, he was pretty sure his

Queen of the Hop could tell them exactly where the blue topaz beetles were if she'd just look.

He wanted to be a toad again. To feel the mud of the pond under his belly. To cram a night crawler into his mouth. To zot low-flying moths in the moonlight.

He thought he knew how to become a toad again. And he had to trust Seer's prophecy that if he kissed the Queen of the Hop, Tumbledown would be saved. Maybe, since she had kissed him first, Toadville was already safe. But he planned to kiss her back, just to be sure. And once he became a toad again, he thought he knew how to get home— if he was right and this girl lived near Toadville-by-Tumbledown.

Eventually, he heard the rock-and-roll music start up. He followed it to where he found lots of humans dancing and eating. It made him sick with longing for the feasts at Tumbledown. Night-smacky-goo. Slug antennae. Shyly shaking pea pods.

He hoped the toads were still there. That he wasn't too late.

A human touched his arm. "Are you registered?"

He just wanted to dance with the Queen of the Hop.

"If you're registered, you should have a name tag," she said.

"Hey, *there* you are!"

It was the queen. She grabbed his hand, and a current shot straight through him and made his freckles pop.

"He's with me," the Queen of the Hop told the name tag human.

"You look really pretty," Tad said. "This is for you." He hung the garland over her head.

"Oh!" she said. "It's beautiful."

The band broke into "Peggy Sue," and her crown blazed in the light as he took her hand.

Taylor stepped and twirled, taking her lead from Tad. It was almost as if they'd danced together before. He swung her arms and did a fancy bouncing step that she tried to follow.

Her dad worked the drums. Taylor's crown

tumbled off, and somebody picked it up and set it on a table.

When the song ended, everybody applauded everybody else. Taylor waved at her parents. They laughed and waved back. Somebody handed her the crown, which she put back on her head.

"Here," Tad said straightening it. Then he turned pink under his freckles.

She led Tad over to the tables. "Are you hungry or thirsty?" she asked.

"Thirsty," he said, picking up a bottle of water and pouring it over his head. "Ahhhh," he sighed. "That feels good."

What an odd boy! Laughing, she dumped a bottle over her own head, hearing the bottle gurgle, and feeling the little slops of icy wetness on her hot, sweaty scalp. It ran behind her ears and down her neck and into her clothes, and felt really, really good. "Whee!" she said, throwing her arms up. She'd never said *whee* before.

The boy took her hand and led her toward the

door. "Let's go look for your toad. Where did you last see him?"

Taylor glanced over her shoulder and caught her mother's eye, then made walking motions with her fingers and pointed to Tad. Her mother nodded.

"You know. Backstage where the dance competition was this afternoon."

As they rode the elevator up to the seventh floor, a man looked at them for a long minute, and then turned to stare politely at the panel of numbers. Taylor didn't care. Being soaking wet and wearing a crown wasn't a bad thing. Actually, it was a really fun thing.

After they got off the elevator, Tad said, "When you get home, don't forget to look for the blue topaz beetles."

"But I've never seen any before." And she knew every inch of Mr. Dennis's old field.

"They like rotting wood," he said. "Remember that."

She nodded.

"So will you look again?"

241

"Okay," she said, laughing.

"Promise?"

He was really interested in those beetles. "Promise."

"Here," he said, handing her the card with the picture of the blue topaz beetle on it. "Take this. You can talk to those people if you find the beetle."

She put it in her skirt pocket. "Now can we look for my toad?"

"Sure," he said.

In the room where the competition had been held, the lights were dim. "It's going to be hard to see," she said. "Be careful not to step on him. He's very small. I wish we had a flashlight."

"I could start over there," the boy said, pointing to where some chairs were stacked, "and you could start over there, and we could meet in the middle."

That was a good plan. In Taylor's corner, somebody had just shoved miscellaneous things into a pile. An empty backpack—which she searched because it could be a good hiding place. A cookie package with crumbs in the bottom. She peered carefully into the shadows where the wall met the floor. A tiny toad would blend in well there.

She and the boy were working their way toward each other. When they met in the middle, he said, "Anything?"

She shook her head. "Nothing." She felt sad, but she also felt kind of tingly, like lightning was about to strike.

"I know he's here someplace." The boy's face glowed. Taylor knew what he was going to do.

Kia had kissed a boy on a field trip and said it was mainly sticky.

Taylor shut her eyes. Kissing was like having goldfish flittering around in your tummy. Like stepping out of your skin and becoming something else. She felt the space around her changing.

When the kiss was over, she kept her eyes closed for a long time, just standing there. It hadn't been the least bit sticky like Kia said.

Had the boy liked it too? Had he kissed anybody before? She hoped he hadn't.

Finally, she opened her eyes.

Where had he gone? "Tad?" she called.

Maybe he was embarrassed. "I liked the kiss," she announced loudly into the shadows. Probably she wasn't supposed to say that.

There was no answer.

It was kind of creepy being backstage in the almost-dark by herself. Why would he go off and leave her?

A little *breeping* came from the floor.

She bent down. Could it be?

It could. It was!

"I am so glad to see you!" she said. "You turned up

just in time. We're leaving first thing in the morning. You almost missed your ride to my grandmother's garden."

She felt such relief. She still had a few canned crickets. She could keep him alive until they got home.

"You're going to be so happy there!" she promised him.

He just looked at her, his eyes shining. His body was relaxed when she picked him up and slid him into her pocket.

On the way down to the room where the band was still playing, she looked everywhere for Tad but didn't find him. He couldn't just kiss her and then disappear like a rabbit in a magic act.

She ate some fruit salad and let a little girl wear her crown for a while. Tad had to come back so she could tell him the excellent news about her toad.

But she couldn't find him anywhere.

That night when she was undressing to get ready for bed, she took the card with the beetle on it out of her pocket and zipped it carefully into a compartment of her backpack. The flowers in the garland Tad had given her were starting to turn a little bit brown around the edges, but she didn't want to throw them away. She folded the garland gently and slid it into her backpack too.

Chapter 36

HE'D TRAVELED FOR A LONG TIME in the stuffy darkness of a hard nest. He was jostled, lifted, tilted, banged, and bumped. Sometimes the girl sprinkled some stale little crickets into the nest.

When the cover finally came off and he saw the night sky, Tad nearly fainted with joy. A light warm mist fell on him, and he just sat there soaking it up. It softened his skin and trickled into his cracks. It fluffed him up and made him feel toadly.

The girl lifted him out of the nest. Blurry gray clouds floated near the ground. The wet grass touched his belly, and he made a little hop. Human feet were nearby, but he knew they wouldn't hurt him.

In a clump of clover, he found five ladybugs and a curly, tender earthworm. *Zot, zot, zot* and triple *zot*, just like that!

This place was nice, he could tell. A lot like home. But now he knew how big the world was, and understood that his chances of finding Toadville-by-Tumbledown were slim to none, unless he was right about one important thing: that he and the girl lived in the same garden.

The humans eventually went away, and Tad sat in the clover. He could see a pond down the bank, its surface dancing with raindrops. It could be his pond. It looked like his pond.

And then he saw Cold Bottom Road on the other side of the clover patch.

Tad began to hop faster, feeling the pollen cling to his wet body. There were dried lilac petals under the bush just where he might find them. And then, to his right, a bit up the hill, was the outline of Toadville-by-Tumbledown. And just beyond it lurked the grim shadow of Rumbler.

But thank the green grass. Oh, thank the green grass. His home was still here!

"Hello!" he called. "Hello!"

A handful of young hoppers were out gathering night crawlers in the rain. "Tad? Is that you?" somebody called.

"It's me," he cried. "I'm back! I'm home!"

The news spread quickly, and toads came tumbling out of Toadville-by-Tumbledown, hopping up Cold Bottom Road.

"We thought something had happened to you!" Tad couldn't tell the voices apart, they came so fast. "We thought we'd never see you again."

Well, he thought he'd never see *them* again either. But here he was. Tad felt as if all the joy in the world glowed inside him.

The clamor continued until an old toad came out to greet him officially. "Welcome home, Tad," he said, his voice deep and hoarse.

Where was Seer? Why didn't the young hoppers go get him and bring him out?

"What took you so long to get back?" somebody demanded. "Where's Buuurk?"

"Buuurk was very brave," Tad said, seeing Anora in the crowd. She was beside Shyly. "He gave his life trying to help me kiss the queen. He was taken up into the Great Cycle. I went on."

The toads looked at him, their eyes shining in the rain. Someone called, "Buuurk was very brave." Anora said, "He was a great singer."

"He was a good friend," somebody else added.

"He was my best friend." Tad felt the empty space beside him just as sharply as he felt the jewel of dreams growing behind his eyes.

"But did you kiss the queen?" one of the old toads asked. "Are we saved?"

"Yes," he said.

Rain dripped from the tree overhead. Otherwise Tumbledown was silent, and Toad wondered if he'd even spoken.

Then the toads broke into shouts. "We're saved! We're saved! He kissed the Queen of the Hop!"

"I'd like to talk to Seer," Tad said when the ruckus had died down.

The silence became as thick as the misty sky. Finally Anora said, "We celebrated his lifting up into the Great Cycle two moonrises ago. We lined the hall with purple phlox. We remembered his prophecies and his wisdom."

Tad felt as if a big rock had fallen on him.

After a while, a chant began very quietly. "Long live the Seer, long live the Seer." All of the toads were looking at him.

Chapter 37

IT HAD ONLY BEEN TEN DAYS since she'd seen her grandmother, but Taylor felt as if she'd been gone for months. Her grandmother looked thinner. But her hug was as good as ever.

"We brought you a ton of stuff," Taylor told her. "Wait till you see."

All the souvenirs were in a big black canvas tote with RENO written in rhinestones. Taylor's mom put it on the table.

"Now, this is the first thing." Taylor took out a CD of Ryan and the Rompers. "This is Mom and Dad's band." She put it on the table in front of Eve. "And look. They had this up during the whole festival." She unrolled the poster she had seen the first night of her dad on drums and her mother singing.

Her grandmother smoothed back the curling edges of the poster, then looked at Taylor. Her eyes were pleased. "I think you had fun."

"Well, yes. But look at what I bought for you. With my own money."

Her grandmother unwrapped the T-shirt that Taylor had rolled carefully in tissue paper and tied with ribbon.

"Do you like it?" Taylor asked, her fingers crossed.

Eve held the T-shirt against her front and looked down at the toad logo. "I love it! Thank you, Taylor. Did you see John Verdun in the hotel?"

Taylor shook her head.

"I saw him entering the lobby with his entourage one night," her dad said. "And I heard he dropped another billion or two on his ecology foundation."

"Put the shirt on," Taylor urged her grandmother. "We can take some pictures. Then we can add them to the album you gave me before we left."

"I can't believe you kept all those old pictures and clippings," Taylor's mom said.

Eve smiled. "They were happy times. Most of them."

Well, of course, it hadn't been happy when Taylor's grandfather got killed so young.

"It's happy music," Taylor's dad said. "Come on, Taylor, show Eve your crown and sash. I've gotta get going."

Was she hearing stuff, or had her dad called her Taylor? She was just starting to like Peggy Sue.

She took the sparkly tiara out of her tote and handed it to her grandmother. "It's kind of big," she explained. "It slides off my head."

Her grandmother turned it so the stones caught the morning sunlight. "It will fit better next year."

"And here's the sash," Taylor said, spreading out the wide red satin ribbon that proclaimed her the Queen of the Hop.

"Look, I hate to say this, but I've really got to hurry," her dad said.

"Me too," her mom added. "Stacks of files will

be towering on my desk. What about we take some pictures first, though?"

"Outside. In the garden," Taylor said. She knew there was no stopping a parent in a hurry. This morning they'd turned on their BlackBerrys, laptops, pagers, beepers, and whiners.

As they went out, Taylor saw the earthmoving machine parked by the old tumbledown shed. She'd glimpsed it in the rain last night. She could still try to save the pond by talking about it on television, but she understood that you couldn't always make things be the way you wanted them to be.

She said to her grandmother, "Maybe we'll see my toad. Did you hear us last night when we came to turn him out into the grass? It was after midnight. That was my special present. I'll tell you all about it later."

Off the back deck, the billowing white baby's breath was almost up to Taylor's waist. "Whoa! That's gotten big. Let's take our pictures standing by that."

So they took pictures of Taylor in her crown and sash standing by the baby's breath. Taylor in her crown and sash, standing between her parents. Taylor and Eve in their matching toad shirts.

Then Taylor took pictures of her grandmother and her parents. In the last one, Taylor's mom wore Taylor's rhinestone crown, and her dad wore the red sash.

"Wait! Don't go away," Taylor said, after she snapped it. "We need the hula hoop."

She ran to the car and got it and hung it around her dad's neck along with the sash.

"Now, that's a picture!"

Her mother took off the crown, her dad lost the sash and hula hoop, and they were gone before Taylor could say *rock and roll*.

And now, finally, Taylor had her grandmother to herself.

They sat down in the grass. Eve hugged her knees, and Taylor copied her grandmother. She leaned against her side. Her grandmother put her arm around Taylor. They still fit like a lock and key.

Down the hill, paddling ducks made Vs on the pond. A cawing crow flew from one mulberry tree to another. Clematis sprawled down the pond bank and grew up on supports. Daylilies caught the sun.

Her grandmother squeezed her. "Tell me every little detail of the trip."

Taylor did, trying to leave nothing out. All about the toad and the dance contest and Diana, last year's queen, and Number 11. About Tad and how he was a little odd, but also nice, and really into the environmental thing. "I poured water over my head the last night," Taylor confessed. "Because he did it. And it was fun." Later, she might tell her grandmother about the kiss.

Eve smiled.

Taylor gazed over the field. From where she sat now, things looked undisturbed. But down the hill, the woods were all torn up. She'd seen it this morning. It made her heart hurt. But if her grandmother could survive whatever was going to happen, Taylor could too.

That afternoon while her grandmother was napping, Taylor walked down to the pond. She lay on the dock and stared up at the clouds, then turned onto her stomach and stared into the water. A school of little fish, their bodies almost clear, shifted and darted. She and Kia had lain here for hours last summer, waiting for fish to swim into their nets. This would be the very last summer. Actually, it could be the last day. She shut her eyes, trying to store everything she loved about the pond in her memory.

She opened her eyes when a heron came in for a landing, its body a T-shape as it dropped its long legs. A fish leaped, sending circles across the pond. Taylor bounced the toes of her sandals against the dock, then quit, wanting the world to be totally quiet. She could hear the little waves making their way to shore, then finally that stopped, and all she could hear was her blood moving around inside.

But then a bullfrog began its silly thrumming call, so loud it made her laugh and forget how solemn and sad she had been feeling. Across the pond, another bullfrog spoke. A breeze stirred her bangs. Taylor yawned. She made a cradle with her arms and rested her head against them. She thought of the little toad

she had brought home, and of the boy who had made her promise to look for the blue topaz beetles.

As she walked back up the hill to the house, she stopped at the old tumbledown shed, which was full of rotting wood. She pulled back the clematis vine that curled around the old posts. At first she only saw scurrying ants, but then, near a hole where the wood had rotted almost totally away, she caught a flash. It flew, but not before she saw that it was a little beetle, so bright it looked like a piece of pale blue glass.

Chapter 38

IN THE HALL OF YOUNG HOPPERS, a golden light fell through the translucent pebbles. Usually Seer would be settled on his pile of milkweed fluff, telling his dreams, drawing the young hoppers out to be their best, whatever that was. Buuurk had been his best—a toadly brave and strong friend. Tad still felt lopsided without Buuurk.

"So what did you see out there?" one of the young hoppers asked Tad.

Shyly asked, "How far did you go?"

"Mother Earth is much bigger than what we can see from the top of the mulch pile," Tad told them.

Murmurs of surprise drifted through the toads.

"Did you hop all the way?" someone asked.

"I hopped a lot. And I moved for several sunrises in a roaring stinky thing with a turtle shell on its back. And once I went fast beneath the foot of a small human. I was in many different nests, and some of them moved around."

"What's a roaring stinky thing?"

Tad explained the best he could.

The hoppers gazed at him, their eyes full of dazzlement and doubt.

"I sat among the stars," Tad said, "and looked down on Mother Earth."

"No," several toads said.

"And I could see that much of Mother Earth is already covered."

A tremor went through the hoppers, and some of the younger ones peed.

"Buuurk and I found another toadville too. The toads there were good to us."

After murmurs of amazement, Shyly said, "So, we're not alone."

"Coverings are very close to their toadville," Tad
said.

"Rumbler still has his big stinky feet right by us,"
somebody said. "So how do you know we're saved?"

"Because I kissed the Queen of the Hop," Tad
said. And he could only hope that she would keep
her promise.

Chapter 39

AS SOON AS HER GRANDMOTHER WOKE UP, Taylor said, "Please! Run me home for a minute. I need to get something out of my backpack."

Before Eve could even ask what, Taylor said, "Remember the boy I told you about? Well, we went through this exhibit of creatures that everybody thought had been wiped out forever, but the ones in this display were discovered alive again—just a few of them, so they're still very endangered." She sucked in a breath and tried to explain calmly about the blue topaz beetles and how the boy had made her promise to look for them. And she had seen one just a while ago! "The lady at the exhibit gave us a postcard and said if we ever saw one, to contact the place printed on the back."

She watched her grandmother trying to follow all this.

"And see, if it really is the blue topaz beetle I saw by the old tumbledown shed, then I'll bet the ecology people will be really interested and will want to come here and check it out, because think how totally special it would be! The lady said it was one of the most endangered beetles in the world."

When she paused for breath, her grandmother said, "But Taylor, I've heard there are more than five thousand different kinds of beetles, or something like that. Some of them must look an awful lot alike. And I'll bet there are many blue ones."

Her grandmother was just trying to keep her from being disappointed. "I know. But run me home so I can get the card, okay?"

An hour later, she was back at Eve's, talking on the telephone to someone who wanted a ton of information. What did the beetle look like? Where did

Taylor live? Exactly. In terms of miles and directions. Eve had to help her with that. What was the history of the land? How had it been used? Her grandmother had to help her with that too.

Well, truthfully, she had seen it for less than a minute, but she just *knew* it was the blue topaz beetle, so she used the postcard a little to help her describe it.

"Hmmmmm," the person on the phone said. "I think we'd like to send out an entomologist. Just to have a look, you know. The chances are one in a billion. Probably less."

"Well, you have to hurry," Taylor said. "The place is going to be turned into a strip mall. Some of the woods have already been knocked down, and there's a big earthmoving machine parked right by where I saw the beetle. Right by it!"

There was a long silence on the other end, then the voice asked Taylor to hold for a couple of minutes while she checked the availability of an expert.

Taylor felt herself gripping the phone, staring out the window at the tumbledown shed, hoping she was in time. Her grandmother made a cup of coffee, poured Taylor some milk, and got down a bag of cookies.

Finally, the person came back on the line. "We happen to have someone at the university near you. He's an expert in temperate zone beetles, and he says he can visit the area where you think you might have a sighting. He can be there in two hours. Will you be available to take him to the exact spot?"

"Oh yes!" Taylor said. "In two hours," she whispered to Eve. "The bug person will be here in two hours."

She and Eve sat on the deck eating cookies and keeping watch. "If anybody tries to move that machine before he gets here," Taylor vowed, "I'll lie down in front of it."

Her grandmother smiled. "That's what we did when I was a girl protesting Vietnam," she said.

Taylor felt like she could hardly breathe. She had almost given up hope, and now that it was back, it filled her to the brim.

"What do you think will happen if there really are blue topaz beetles living in the tumbledown shed?" she asked.

Even Eve acted truly hopeful, though Taylor could tell she was trying not to. "First of all, there will be a lot of publicity. It will get people talking. It will get environmentalists interested in the acreage."

"Maybe that rich guy's ecology foundation will buy it," Taylor said. "Isn't he the second-richest man in the world? Maybe he'll buy it to save the beetles."

"John Verdun." Her grandmother smiled. "You never know."

Chapter 40

THE LOAMY TUNNEL had fallen around Tad during the long night of winter and padded him like a brown blanket. But now the earth was stirring. And even three feet down, the old hopper felt it.

Maybe it was footsteps in the garden, or the deep, seepy drip of warm rain. Maybe it was the chorus of spring peepers.

Tad stirred too. With the ancient toady wisdom, he knew the days were getting warm and sunny up top.

Tad woke up half frozen to his center from a long season of sleep. Sluggishly, he scootched upward through the sand and clay and veins of rotting roots. Moisture soaked through his dry, papery skin.

Near the surface, Tad tried a little hop. But it was lopsided and feeble—just a lurch, really, that flopped him half out of his hole. Using his rear diggers, he scrambled the rest of the way out and sat in the April sun for a while.

He could no longer see the sun, but he could feel it. Tad's eyes had turned milky over the years, like crystal balls. But although he was blind, he could still see many things.

He sat as still as the clod of earth he might have been mistaken for. A newly awakened young hopper would come along soon and lead him back to Toadville-by-Tumbledown. That was the place he was headed. That was the place he was *always* headed this time of year.

How many springs had Tad come to life again?

He wasn't sure and couldn't say. But many.

He sensed the girl nearby, as he often did. He couldn't see her anymore, but he knew when she was there. She still warmed him like the sun, tugged him like the moon, and made his heart dance like the stars.

Today, Taylor was picking oxeye daisies by the tumbledown. As she pushed her hair back from the wind, her ruby ring that Eve had given her for her fourteenth birthday caught the sunlight.

"Pretty!" Kia exclaimed, looking at it.

She and Kia were on the committee for the eighth grade end-of-year party, and Taylor was supposed to bring flowers for the refreshment table—which was why she was picking her grandmother's daisies.

"So who do you think you'll dance with?" Kia asked, plucking the petals off a daisy and naming two boys she thought were cute.

Taylor shrugged. There *was* Carter Harris. He was cute, and he'd called her twice already. But even after three years, Taylor still compared all boys to the one who'd helped her look for her toad in Reno. The one who had told her about the blue topaz beetles. The one who had helped her save the pond.

The ecology people had located fourteen blue topaz beetles in the rotting timbers of the old tumbledown shed. It had all been on TV, better than Taylor had hoped—the beautiful beetles, Taylor, and Eve. Several ecologists and entomologists. Mr. Verdun, the second-richest man in the world. Even the owner of the pond and woods. In front of the cameras, he acted like he'd bought the land *because* it had a few wonderful shiny blue beetles. And he had happily sold it for a ton of money to the Verdun Foundation as a land preserve. He didn't say a word about the woods he had turned topsy-turvy and the pond he had been planning to drain.

Any time Taylor saw Mr. Verdun on television, she always searched the crowd for Tad. She knew his family was active in trying to save the environment, and she thought she might glimpse him. She never did.

But she would never forget him. Not ever. Sometimes when she was in her grandmother's garden, she got this strange feeling. . . . Taylor laid down the tulips so she could pull up her hood. And that's when she saw the small toad right by her left shoe.

She studied the little guy, paying attention to the pattern of his warts and the size of his eyes. He *looked* like the toad she had brought back from Reno and turned loose in her grandmother's garden.

Her grandmother called from the deck. Taylor turned and saw Eve pointing to the pond. Taylor stood up to look. A family of ducks was making a pattern of rippling V-shapes. Each

spring, the pond seemed a little smaller to Taylor, but no less magical. Most years, a groundhog paraded her babies for Eve and Taylor to admire. Every April, Eve and Taylor planted seeds with names like *nasturtium* and *chocolate morning glory*. And always, she was on the lookout for her special toad.

A gust of wind caught Taylor's hood, and the breeze brought her back to reality. She still had so many things to do.

"It's time to go," she told Kia.

She moved carefully away, trying not to disturb the little toad or the earth around him.

Acknowledgments

To my good friend Carol Gorman for having long every-other-Saturday phone calls in the early days of the story.

To my writers' group (Jan Blazanin, Eileen Boggess, and Rebecca Janni) for reading version after version of the manuscript.

To my agent, Susan Cohen, for finding a good home for *The Hop*.

To my editor, Abby Ranger, for knowing where the story needed to go and guiding me there.

To my granddaughter Lizzie for helping me see small things in the garden.